Murder
Among the Mannequins

D1607749

Penelope Clifton

Murder Among the Mannequins
Pondsprings Publishing
ISBN: 978-1-7941-1096-0
Copyright © 2019 by Penelope Clifton
All rights reserved.

Acknowledgements

As with all books, this one would not exist in its present form without the help of a tribe. My thanks go to Aldema Ridge for getting me started and keeping me going, to Sherri Mayer for valuable critiques, to Deborah Dove for her eagle proofing eye and to friends in the Chesapeake Chapter of Sisters in Crime, including Donna Andrews and Eileen McIntire for their guidance and tips, and especially Barb Goffman for her superb editing. Thanks also to my Artist's Way group, Susan, Gayl, Mimi, Katie, Becky, Barbara, Sandy, and Salley who are my Believing Mirrors and gave me encouragement at just the right times. Thanks to my son Tim for the cover design. Also to my family and friends for believing I could do it, and for putting up with hearing about the process for as long as it took.

Murder Among the Mannequins

Table of Contents

Murder Among the Mannequins

Chapter 28

Murder Among the Mannequins

Murder Among the Mannequins

Chapter 28 176

Murder Among the Mannequins

Chapter 28 176
Chapter 29 183
Chapter 30 190
Chapter 31 197
Chapter 32 204

Murder Among the Mannequins

Chapter 1

*O*ther people work in modern offices with matching furniture. I work in an old mill with body parts. Cases of glass eyeballs. Vinyl heads. Molds of arms and legs and hands. I'd never intended to be second in command at my family's mannequin-manufacturing company, yet here I am, sketching a costume for our current job.

"Helll-ooo," my friend Rose Ebaugh called from the front door, breaking my concentration. Rose owned the studio next door, where she made reproduction vintage clothing. She was developing a pretty good following for her fashions from the Roaring Twenties through the 1940s. She called her company Vintage Dresses, which was an accurate but unimaginative name. She saw customers by appointment only, so I never knew when she would be in. Hers was the only other company that shared the second floor of the old mill building with our company, Montgomery Mannequins. I had only known Rose for two years, since she relocated her workshop from her nearby rowhouse into Harbor Mill, but I knew her well enough to silently mouth her next words as she spoke them, even though I couldn't yet see her.

"God, those hands, Laney!"

Rose's shoes made a shuffling sound as she took the quickest route from the front door back to my design room, which took her straight through the Haunted House, as she referred to our large storage area. Her footsteps—and her humming—grew louder as she shuffled past the office door and through the storage area. It was dimly lit from meager track lighting overhead, which did nothing to diminish the haunted house feeling. The floor creaked as Rose circumnavigated the shelves of vinyl heads and molds of hands. I knew the case of glass eyeballs stared at her as she walked by. Not even the quilts I hung on the walls did much to soften the décor.

"I can't believe he made his clients walk through this haunted house to get to his cave," Rose mumbled just loud enough for me to hear. The "he" she referred to was my grandfather, Albert Montgomery, originator of the company. The cave she referred to was where I was sitting: a tiny, dark room where Grandpa Albert could squirrel himself away to create his prototype sketches, and which I now used as my design room.

Rose always shuddered at our storage area; I knew she thought of it as archaic remnants of creepy miscellany. To me, it was tools of the trade—head molds, glass eyeballs, and vinyl body parts: torsos and limbs, walls of disembodied vinyl hands and feet. Grandpa Albert had always displayed castings from the molds on the storage area walls outside his cave. These walls became his makeshift showroom, an index of hand and foot choices, so to speak, for those clients who came to visit. Once Elise took over, she never changed it. We were used to stepping over boxes with hands and feet sticking out of them at awkward angles. But to others, I suppose, it looked like a Civil War hospital tent. Minus the blood, of course. Since I now used Grandpa Albert's tiny office, aka the cave, for my design room, I had grown accustomed to walking past body parts lining the walls. But Rose never had.

I glanced up and saw Rose grimace as she reached my design room. She stood under the arch of limbs hanging on the wall above my doorway.

"Oh God, Laney. All those hands," she said and shook her head. Of all the body parts hanging on the walls, I knew the hands bothered Rose the most. Probably because she worked with hers and thought of them like her needle and thread—tools of her trade, not disembodied body parts.

My nose was buried in my sketchbook. "I'll be right with you, Rose. I want to finish this before I lose the image." I was buried in the mass of papers and books laying open around me. Three of Grandpa Albert's old pattern books lay open on the drafting table behind me.

My design room is where I lay out plans and research costumes for the figures we make. Grandpa Albert called them mannequins, hence the name Montgomery Mannequins. People outside the industry call them dummies. But ever since I accompanied Grandpa Albert to the National History Museum in New York to see his mannequins in dioramas, I had called them museum figures. I was five, and I was in awe, and a little afraid, of these creations that Grandpa made. They held an air of reverence for me then, and this cozy little room still did now. It had been Grandpa Albert's office when he started the business. The self-contained room was carved out of a front corner of the main office but was only accessible from the storage area and therefore had no windows. As a child, I loved it. If you closed the door, no one knew you were in there. As an adult, I loved it because I could spin around on the stool and reach anything I needed from the many built-in cabinets and shelves.

I was squeezed just inside the doorway of the tiny room on a stool facing the side wall. I had to balance my sketchbook on a small angle board, which perched on my knees and rested against the wall. There was no room for a full drafting table.

"I can't believe you really use all these old, dusty books," Rose said, looking at the floor-to-ceiling bookshelves and map cabinets. I turned my head to see her grinning and taking up most of the doorway, at least the width of it, if not the height.

In some ways, Rose spanned three centuries: she looked like a nineteenth-century woman, rugged and stocky; she loved mid-twentieth century fashions; but she was trapped in the twenty-first century. She was built more like a sturdy pioneer woman than a dress designer, and wore loose comfort clothes like the denim jumper she had on today. At only five feet tall, Rose called herself a typical South Baltimore girl. She claimed she had a perfect muumuu body. She had never been able to fit ready-to-wear clothes, and she always joked that she was a perfect size thirteen. She'd called her first dressmaking business Lucky Thirteen and specialized in designs for the hard-to-fit bodies. I don't think she'd been a size thirteen in a long time, but she knew her trade. It was what first drew us together: the fact that we were both in "body-building" businesses.

"Are you ready to see your twin?" I said, referring to the figure she had commissioned us to make for her. I stood up, switching off the work light and turning to her in the doorway. I stopped.

"Oh good, you've brought the dress!"

Rose was grinning and carefully holding up the garment bag next to her short frame, not wanting to wrinkle its precious contents.

"C'mon into the clean room. Burl's not quite done yet, but I asked him to bring your figure up so you could see her."

I followed Rose out through the storage area and into the next room. She kept her head straight, clearly avoiding the case of glass eyeballs staring at her, some crossed, some looking at the ceiling, one shattered.

"Don't forget to wipe your feet," I said, shuffling my shoes on the doormat inside the clean room. It was a struggle to keep the sawdust out. Rose was rolling her eyes, but she obliged. She was used to my fastidiousness when it came to keeping this room neat.

The room was so large it dwarfed the eight-by-sixteen-foot worktable in the center of the room. It was the one area I kept pristine. This room was the last stop in the production of the figures, after they came up from the back two production rooms, Burl's workshop, and the casting room. Here the figures were finished, dressed, photographed, and prepared for shipment. The interior walls were lined with shelves and everything was in its place—the tools, nuts, bolts, padding, and extra hands and feet. I'd learned long ago that keeping a clean workspace was paramount to shipping a quality product. When the figures left this room they went to their new homes in some of the most prestigious history museums in the world; into military dioramas, historical houses, and occasionally corporate visitor centers.

I didn't need to direct Rose to her figure. Straight ahead, standing in front of the worktable was Rose's twin, and she came nose to nose with her and froze. I wasn't sure if she was pleased or frightened, but this was not the reaction I had hoped for.

Chapter 2

"I feel like I'm looking in a mirror!" Rose looked into the light brown eyes. She reached out to touch the straight brown hair that mimicked her boyish cut. "The hair looks like it's growing from the scalp!"

"We aim for realism," I said, feeling pleased for the hair artist who had implanted the hair, then cut and styled it. I'd be sure to pass on Rose's compliments.

"It's great! It looks just like me—but better somehow!" Rose circled the figure.

"You have Burl to thank for that." I didn't add that he knew just where to shave off a few pounds, while keeping a close likeness. He had become very good at his job in the five years he'd been with us.

My stomach rumbled. I was hungry, but I didn't hurry Rose. I was enjoying her reaction.

"Let's put the dress on her. Let's see how she looks," Rose said, pulling a gorgeous purple dress out of the plastic garment bag. It was that deep, rich shade that I thought of as royal purple. I removed one of the figure's arms, and we slipped the dress easily over its head. I slid the free arm down into the empty sleeve and locked it back onto the figure. The dress was one of Rose's classic 1930s tea-length gowns, and it hit the figure perfectly, several inches above the ankle. The left side of the bodice was overlaid with patterned silk, a good design element that added color and vertical lines. I took a close look at the pin anchoring the low V-neckline.

"Rose, do you know what this pin is made of? It looks like sapphires and diamonds."

Rose smiled. "The purple stones are iolite and the clear ones are crystal. I asked Catherine to make me something special for this dress, and she sure came through. Isn't it gorgeous?" I knew Catherine was the jeweler who subleased the back room of Rose's dress shop for her studio. I hadn't known her long, but I liked her very much. She hadn't the airs that I'd expected, knowing she was from one of Baltimore's iconic families. Catherine mostly worked on commissioned pieces, but had a few one-of-a-kind pieces for sale in Rose's display case. I always looked at the display case whenever I stopped in to Vintage Dresses.

"It's perfect! I have to admit, Rose, when you told me you were incorporating Catherine's jewelry into your dresses, I was a little worried. It sounded…well, tacky, combining jewelry right into the dresses."

"Like East Bawl-a-mer?" Rose joked. She was referring to the reputation of the neighborhood before the yuppies started moving in and the prices went up.

I turned the figure, checking the fit of the dress. The lines worked perfectly on the mannequin. The shoulders fit without pulling too tightly, and it skimmed the hips with enough ease to be comfortable, but close enough to be flattering. I pinched in a bit of fabric at the waist, just where Burl had shaved off a few pounds. Now it looked perfect.

"It needs a slight alteration here. How about if I do it for you tonight? I know you have a couple of other dresses you need to finish today for your bridal show."

"Oh thanks, Laney. You're one of the few people I would let near one of my gowns with scissors. But be careful with it. Don't trim the seam too closely."

I pinched in a half-inch at both sides of the waistline and anchored two straight pins. "I'm going to put the dress back in the costume room right now. Let's go eat. I'm starved!"

"I'll need that dress tomorrow, you know," Rose reminded me.

"It'll be done. In fact, I'll deliver the whole figure to you at the Redwood Hotel," I called over my shoulder. I knew this was the first bridal show where Rose was exhibiting her wares, and a little handholding was in order.

"Really? Oh, that would be great. I need to set the booth up by 5:00 p.m."

Returning from the costume room, I reassured her, "I'll give you a call in the afternoon. Don't worry." My stomach rumbled so loudly, I was sure she'd heard it.

"Let's go to Annie's for lunch. I'm just gonna go grab my sweater. I'll meet you downstairs."

"I'm in!" I headed into the office to retrieve my coat. Elise was at her desk sorting through the mail. Her nameplate, which was quite long since it read Elise Montgomery Carrington, was balanced on the stack of mail as a paperweight.

"Laney, Burl almost has your new mannequin ready. I want you to take a look at it."

I turned my back to Elise and reached for my coat.

"I keep telling you, I'm not ready!" I knew she didn't even hear me. Again. I slung my coat over my shoulder and stormed out of the office and back into the clean room, where Burl was lifting a new figure onto the large central worktable.

"Here she is, Laney. I couldn't wait to finish her off . . . so to speak." He put his power tools aside and stepped his large, solid frame back from the table so I could see the body. "I know you didn't want me to do this, but you know I had to do what the boss said."

"Oh!" I looked down and stared into my own face.

The mannequin's bright green eyes stared back at me. I didn't think my eyes were quite that shade of green, prompting me to glance briefly at the mirror on the wall. The figure's dark auburn curls coming strand by strand from the scalp amazed me, even after all these years of being around realistic mannequins. I bristled at the hint of gray blended in at the temples. I frowned at the crow's feet around her eyes.

"Oh, look at those freckles!" I touched my nose, where makeup covered mine. Gazing over the length of her body, I noticed her fingertips even showed fingerprints. Were they mine? I gave a shudder and felt my neck and cheeks turn warm when I saw that Burl got the proportions of my breasts and hips correct, even the extra bit around my waist. My stomach was tied in a knot, and for a moment I felt lightheaded and leaned against the worktable.

Burl muttered, "I know. It was really creepy building *you*."

"No, no, it's okay. You've done a good job with her," I managed to squeak out. Too good, I thought. I was used to working with realism, just not my own. Realism of famous people, long dead, like Einstein or Lincoln, or Mr. J. C. Penney, or famous contemporary people who want a clone, but not me. Now I knew what Rose felt when she first saw her figure.

I headed back to the cherry Victorian wardrobe in the costume room to retrieve the dress that would truly finish off my figure. The costume room, set along the outer wall of the clean room, was the size of a large walk-in closet, and made good use of the windows, which provided plenty of light for storing and steaming and otherwise preparing and fitting the figures' clothing.

The tapping of Elise's trademark high heels on the lacquered wooden floors announced her arrival. "Is 'Miss Cookie' ready?" She had a smile that I tried not to interpret as a smirk. "I know this one was a quick job. Good work, Burl!" Elise said, fingering the sequined fabric hanging over my arm.

"She's almost ready," I snapped, standing up the figure and slipping the teal, beaded dress over its head, careful not to disturb the perfectly implanted and casually coifed hair. "I don't know why you call her Miss Cookie," I told Elise, shaking my head to mask the shudder that escaped. Like I didn't know what she was doing, even if she had given the figure a code name.

"Are you all right?" Elise asked.

"I'm fine," I answered gruffly. I'd be damned if I'd let her know this creeped me out. The little slip of a dress slid over the body. *A little too little*, I thought of the dress. I couldn't help laughing, "Well, that was one of my quickest dressing jobs ever." The gown hung delicately from the mannequin's shoulders, lightly skimming the body all the way to the floor. Burl had worked his magic again to shed a few pounds. I wished I looked that good.

"That teal dress looks stunning against her hair. You should think about coloring yours to hide the gray." Elise ran her hand from the mannequin's head down the length of its arm. I shuddered again, feeling ghostly fingertips on my own arm.

"It's *my* hair," I muttered. "If you want it to look like me, the silver flecks stay."

"Well, you should be flattered anyway."

"Well, I'm not. I don't know why you had to make this one of me. I know you loved assuming command from Grandpa Albert, but you know I'm not ready to take over the business."

"Laney, you're making too much of this." Elise put her coffee mug into the microwave, and hit "warm." She turned to face me, knowing I'd have a reply.

"Now you're sounding like my mother," I mumbled.

"I *am* your mother."

"Not on work time." I rarely needed to remind her of the ground rules we'd set up when I agreed to work here. In fact, she was usually better at remembering them than I was, ever since she broke her leg three years ago and I'd agreed to move home and help. *Help* with the family business, not run it.

Recently, Elise was pushing me harder to take the reins of the company. *She* was ready to move on, but I wasn't. In the early years, Grandpa Albert had made a figure of himself, a doppelganger, to promote sales for his fledgling business. Elise always knew she would take over the business from her father, and had looked forward to creating a figure of herself. Now it was my turn. *She* thought. She was making plans for opening a restaurant in her retirement in Carter's Village, not far from her house. I was keeping plans as they were—with her running Montgomery Mannequins and me helping out while pursuing my real passion, making art quilts. I looked again at my figure.

"Relax! She looks great." Elise looked at the mannequin too. Her clipped, professional tone had returned. Waving her hand in the air, she turned on her heel, coffee in hand. "And we need it for advertising. End of story."

"But I really don't want one of me."

Elise responded much too quickly, "It looks great. Just like you'll look when you shed those ten pounds you've been battling."

Experience told me it was useless to respond. She was gone. I was always amazed that my diet struggles were more a source of concern to my mother than they were to me. That, and her interest in my friend

Dale Adams, when she used that tone, "your *friend.*" It made me roll my eyes. I'd known Dale since I was a kid. He'd done well and made it to the rank of homicide detective, and he was "easy on the eyes" as Grandma Emily used to say. I knew Elise would like to have him as her son-in-law, even though he was closer to her age than mine. Other than that, she was pretty good about butting out of my life. I just wished she'd totally butt out, and take the whole company with her. I'd been avoiding having another conversation about this sore subject, but it was looking like I'd need to have it again. Soon.

I stared at the figure that I was trying to think of as a non-specific figure, a non-ident. Just a mannequin, custom-made for a client by letting them choose the features like a Mr. Potato Head toy. I'd made figures for years, borrowing features from myself and others. So what was bugging me about this replica of me?

I was feeling boxed in, and the box was getting smaller.

Chapter 3

*T*here's one thing about the elevator in the mill. One big thing. Sometimes it gets stuck. Well, not stuck exactly, it just decides not to work. Not often and not for long, but I'd hold my breath every time I hit the button. Now was no exception, and I was glad to see it was behaving.

Jacket in hand, I stepped out on the first floor and caught Rose's eye as she sat on a bench next to the front door. I collided with Carlos, Harbor Mill's newest tenant. He stopped abruptly, his camera bag sliding from his shoulder. I hadn't seen him since he signed a lease with us and moved in a few days ago. All I knew was he planned to open a photography studio on the first floor. He'd apparently lost his lease in his old building near the Inner Harbor. Elise's underground network of Baltimore commercial property owners had told her the new owner had tripled the rents to force out the current tenants, mainly artists. He was probably turning the building into high-end condos. It was a problem for the arts scene all over the Inner Harbor. That's why Elise was planning on renovating the fourth floor, adding more studio space. We knew we'd have tenants clamoring for them. That was another reason I didn't want her to retire. Being a landlord had never been on my bucket list.

"How's it goin'?" he said, nodding, his accent thick.

"Oh, sorry, Carlos. Hey, there's a tenant notice under your door," I alerted him. Carlos nodded and continued down the hall to his first floor studio. "Oh, and Burl wants to talk to you."

"He knows where to find me." I heard an edge to his voice.

"Anything I can do?"

"Nah, jus' some problem we got wit' the guy who's buyin' up all the good studios an' apartments." He said it gruffly, as if he were angry.

"Not you and Elise. You're—how to say—the last bastion," he called.

"What's that about?" Rose stood up from the bench by the front door.

"Beats me. Sounds like the reason Carlos lost his last place. Elise told me the rents are going up in the arts district because of gentrification. Come to think of it, I wonder if that's why Burl has to find a new apartment. I know he's lost his place, and he's having trouble finding one he can afford."

"Is that why you've had a lot of new people move in recently? The mill is filling up," Rose observed. "Your mother had a great idea, converting this old mill into artists' studios and workshops. It's done wonders for my business, moving it out of my house."

"She's always had good timing." *Except when it comes to her retirement.*

Harbor Mill's neighborhood, once considered working-class East Baltimore, was now included inside the expanding boundary of the trendy area known as Canton, on the east side of Baltimore's Inner Harbor.

Young professionals were moving into the area, buying and renovating the townhouses and warehouses. The residences now sported new brick faces, brass lanterns, and rooftop decks.

I had to admit the mill was perfect for small shops and artists' studios. The floor-to-ceiling windows on the north side ensured good light all day, without the direct sunlight that was so detrimental to fabric and paintings. Because of that, the artists in the front studios were willing to overlook the view of the parking lot, literally. There was a small green square behind the building, nestled into the L shape of the building. The square had a tiny sign announcing it was called Harbor Mill Park, although it was hardly big enough to hold more than two benches and a couple of shrubs. Still, it was a welcome bit of green among asphalt and brick, and afforded us a place to have lunch outside on sunny days, with a nice view of Baltimore's Harbor East. Elise never had to advertise. Word spread quickly through the art community whenever there was a studio available. She kept the rent reasonable; it was her way of supporting the arts.

It was a crisp, sunny day as Rose and I walked up Washington Street to Annie's, our favorite neighborhood restaurant and bar. Well, it used to be a bar. Now it was a pub; we knew this because its menu was changing and its prices were climbing up. We passed several blocks of red brick rowhouses. A few residents were outside scrubbing their white marble steps one last time before winter set in. That was a real art in itself, maintaining the famous white marble steps of Baltimore. The Bon Ami and pumice sat proudly on each top step. I was glad the newcomers kept up the tradition. It was one of the things that I loved about the neighborhood.

"I thought Elise was talking about retirement," Rose mused.

"She is. But she says she'd still manage the renovation of the fourth floor."

"You feelin' any more confident 'bout taking over the business?"

"No, I'm not ready for that. At this point, I really don't want the headaches. I just want to work on the figures."

We walked on in silence for a while.

"And my quilts, of course. I've really neglected my quilts. If Elise insists on retiring, I'll just have to hire a business manager if I want time for my quilts." I tried to put that thought out of my head.

Rose and I quickly covered the few blocks to Annie's, walking at a brisk pace to match the fall air. As we neared, the aroma enticed us to walk even faster. Annie's has been a favorite lunch place of locals ever since her father, whom everyone called Pops, opened it in 1965 and named it after his new daughter. The building still clung to the past, maintaining its East Baltimore Formstone™ rowhouse look. The other rowhouses and businesses up and down Washington Street had peeled away the mid-century popular façade and returned the buildings to a nineteenth-century look of old brick and brass lamps. Annie's had made it to the 1950s and stopped.

The place was crowded, but I managed to catch Annie's eye. She swung a beer mug in the air as a kind of acknowledgement. After setting down the beer in front of a customer, she made her way over to us.

That's what I liked about Annie; she still waited tables and knew her regulars by name. And, true to the stereotype of Baltimore waitresses, most everyone was "Hon" to her, whether they were first-timers or she had known them for years; whether they were youngsters or twice her age.

"Hi, Hon. Sorry we're crowded." Flustered, she added, "I mean, I'm not sorry we're crowded. I meant, sorry you hafta' wait." Annie always sounded like she was in a hurry and had her tongue wrapped around a marble with that broad Bawl-mer accent.

"It's okay, Annie. We can wait." I knew she'd find us a table within a few minutes; Annie's was a quick lunch spot for the businesses nearby.

Out of the din came a voice. "Rose?"

We both turned. A man waved us over to his booth. He was distinguished looking, but I suddenly and inexplicably felt cautious. Funny how a split-second glance at someone can categorize him. It was the evenly graying hair and the hand-tailored suit, I realized. And something else, but I didn't know what.

"Kalen! What're you doing here?" Rose walked toward his booth. "I didn't know you knew about Annie's. I'n't it a little far from your office?"

I peered over Rose's shoulder and was surprised to see Catherine Gilbert-Smith at the table. Catherine, of the pin-on-Rose's-dress fame. Of the rents-Rose's-back-room fame. She sat between two men in the horseshoe-shaped booth. Her blond hair and fair complexion belied her Italian heritage.

I nodded to Catherine. I'd only known her for a year or so, but she seemed to be "good people," down to earth, not stuffy.

"Hello, Catherine. I didn't realize you were coming here for lunch. You could have walked over with us." I caught a slight hesitation from Catherine.

"Thanks, but I came from a meeting with a client."

She made quick introductions, pointing toward the man with the graying hair. "Do you know Kalen Farrell? He works at my father's firm."

I knew that Catherine's father was Franklin Gilbert-Smith, co-founder of Gilbert Strickland, Baltimore's premier financial house. It wasn't the largest, but it was the best, and it occupied some prime real estate in the city. All of the old money in Baltimore used them. If you wanted financial advice, you "called Gilbert." He was old school, and his family had hyphenated their name for generations, before it became fashionable. I also knew that Catherine had been invited into the firm, but instead had chosen her own career as an artist, much to her father's disapproval. That's how she ended up sharing Rose's shop, and that's as much as I knew about Catherine. Or her father.

"I'm so happy to meet one of Catherine's friends," Kalen said, standing and firmly taking my hand. His voice was deep and rich, and his hand was pleasantly warm. He knew just how long to grasp mine. *Did this man do everything flawlessly?*

My eyes were glued to Kalen. He was attractive and charismatic, even though he was a good fifteen years my senior. I mentally shook myself. It's not that I was interested in him; it was more like he commanded attention. Something about his eyes; they had a sharpness to them. Kalen was indeed distinguished. Polished. *Too polished*, I thought warily. I had had my fill of men like that.

"Let me introduce Michael Leland. He's with me at Gilbert Strickland." Kalen's voice brought my attention back to the table. I wondered which one was the boss.

Catherine shed a little more light. "Michael's my father's new VP."

"Hello." Michael extended his hand, exuding warmth without using many words. Taking his hand, I inadvertently glanced at his ring finger and noticed it was bare. I quickly looked around to see if Annie had a table for us yet.

"Want to join us? It might be awhile before another table opens up." Michael's voice was deep and soft. Both men towered over Catherine, even while seated. Michael was considerably younger than his colleague, perhaps in his late thirties, but commanded a quiet sort of authority. I felt warmth rising up my neck and fervently hoped it was not visible. I was more surprised than annoyed; I haven't been a kid for a long time, and it surprised me to feel like one.

Rose turned to me. "Would ya mind? Not waitin'? I have a lot to do this afternoon."

"Fine by me." It wasn't really fine, but I was hungry. I felt a little annoyed. I didn't know these men, and I had wanted to talk more with Rose about her trade show, as well as the looming issue of Elise's retirement.

Michael and Kalen both slid over, squeezing Catherine at the head of the horseshoe-shaped banquette. Rose sat down next to Kalen, which left the space next to Michael open. I perched gingerly on the edge of the bench seat. I felt awkward since the booths were not oversized.

"Waitress!" Kalen shouted, and waved Annie over for Rose and me to order.

"I'll have these samwiches out in a jiff, Hon," Annie said after taking our orders. I assumed she was addressing us all and that was the plural "Hon."

Kalen spoke first. "So, what are you lovely ladies up to?" Before I could open my mouth he turned to Rose. "Catherine tells me you have some great new dress designs. You're really keeping her busy making pins. She doesn't even have enough time to —"

Catherine interrupted. "Yes, Rose is giving me so many pieces to design for her dresses, I think she should change her shop's name to 'BeJeweled.'" She smiled at Rose.

Just then, Annie showed up with three Heavy Seas, a local beer. The icy condensation made trails across the table. They were followed by my iced tea and Rose's Diet Pepsi.

Rose took a sip and continued. "Yeah, Catherine does such neat stuff, and I needed a 'hook.' You know, a way for my dresses to stand out from the rest. I mean, *I* know they're good, but when you're a small fish in a big pond, you need some way to bring the fishermen to you!"

Michael looked directly at me. "I've seen the jewelry that Catherine makes. And I've heard about the gowns that Rose makes, but where do you fit in?" His brown eyes were warm and sincere, a nice contrast to Kalen's.

"We're neighbors. In Harbor Mill." I nodded in the general direction of the mill. "My company is Montgomery Mannequins, on the second floor next to Catherine and Rose's space." I didn't mention that I was their landlord. Kalen looked around, and his eyes settled on Catherine. Michael was looking into my eyes, waiting for me to continue. "Right now, I'm making a mannequin for Rose to use this weekend. Actually to display her newest bejeweled creation." I liked the way that sounded and made a mental note to advocate changing the name of Rose's shop from Rose's Vintage Dresses to BeJeweled.

"And Catherine just finished a gorgeous topaz brooch that replicates one in the photo I used to replicate the person. I guess we all work together, in a manner of speaking. I duplicated the woman, in this case, Miss Prudence Suttler, Rose duplicated her gown, and Catherine duplicated her pin. The dress and the pin are exact matches to the reference photo —"

"Oh, let's not talk shop, Laney," Catherine interrupted. I was surprised she was embarrassed to talk about her work. She wasn't usually shy, and this praise was not unfounded.

I pressed on. "Catherine had an old costume pin that had a wonderful faceted glass bead the same color as the topaz brooch I'm copying, so she reworked it for me. That figure is ready to ship in a day or two. It's one of our best figures." I smiled my thanks at Catherine. I looked around and saw that Kalen was not smiling. He was glaring at Catherine.

"I didn't know your *pin* was finished!" he said in a low voice to Catherine.

Chapter 4

Rose's face brightened. "Oh, Catherine, I'd love to take that Miss Prudence dress to my bridal show tomorrow at the Redwood Hotel." Rose looked at me and continued, "But I don't think Laney can have the figure finished by then."

"I'll try, but I'm not making any promises on that one, Rose."

Just then Annie brought the sandwich platters. The crab cake and shrimp salad permeated the air, reminding me I was ravenous. I was grateful for the quick service, and bit into my shrimp salad. I was beginning to feel more and more uncomfortable. I didn't know Michael Leland well enough to be sitting hip to hip with him, and I didn't like how my pulse was racing. I picked up the shrimp that had fallen out of my sandwich and popped it into my mouth.

Kalen and Catherine were deep in a discussion about jewelry finds at street markets in Florence and Rome. I wondered if they traveled together. I turned to Michael and made an effort at conversation, hoping it would make the time go faster.

"So what keeps you busy when you're not at Gilbert Strickland?"

"Construction."

I hate one-word answers. It was as if I had asked him if he liked milk. And it left me puzzled. Didn't Catherine say he was a vice president for Gilbert Strickland?

"You own a construction company?"

Michael chuckled, not unkindly. "No, I have a house in need of it." He took a bite of his sandwich.

"And you're doing it yourself?" I wondered if it was always this hard to get this man to converse. And I wondered why he didn't hire contractors to do the construction for him. Once again, I had finished eating before everyone else, a habit that annoyed me, but no one else seemed to notice. I must have finally touched on Michael's interest, because he launched into what, for him, must have been a long conversation.

"My dad taught me to work with my hands. We'd work on our boat a lot. I used to hate it. Now I find it relaxing and therapeutic. Doing anything with wood. Repairs. Building from scratch."

Kalen shook his head and brought the conversation around to himself. "I don't work with my hands. I work with my head. All the time. Even when I'm not at the office. Especially when I'm not at the office. Working with your hands is for other guys. That's why I got my MBA." He stated it as though any of us had asked. Or cared. Everyone looked at him. I would have said something to him about not caring, but I didn't want to sound as ignorant as he did. Besides, I figured my opinion, or anyone else's, wouldn't carry much weight with him.

Kalen continued, "That's why I'm getting into real estate. This town's a gold mine, especially near the Inner Harbor. Bunch of dumps just ripe for the picking." His voice was louder than necessary, causing several heads to turn toward our table. It was past time to be done with this lunch, I thought, laying down a twenty to cover my order.

"I got this." Kalen reached across the table and pushed the bill back towards me.

As we left the table, Kalen announced, "My car's in the lot. I'll drop you back at the mill." He was looking from Catherine, to Rose, to me. It sounded more like a command than an offer.

"No thanks, we need the exercise," Rose said with a grin.

Speak for yourself, I thought. I would have taken the ride, even from Kalen, but I knew Rose was right. She was a city girl and walked most places. She did own a car, however old and rusted, but dreaded losing her coveted parking spot in front of her rowhouse. I, on the other hand, liked to drive if I had to go more than two blocks.

"No, thanks," I conceded. I knew I could use the exercise.

"Are you coming back to the shop, Catherine?" I invited her to walk with us.

"No, you go on. I've got some errands to run, and I have my car here."

Rose and I started down Washington Street. I heard raised voices, and turned around to see Kalen in the parking lot, in a heated conversation with Catherine. He grabbed her wrist, and just as quickly, she wrenched it away from him. Catherine looked around and caught my eye. I waited, frozen, caught between intervening and ignoring. Kalen got into his Porsche, which made me wonder how he would have given the three of us a ride, and peeled out of the parking lot, so close to us that his bumper brushed my skirt.

Catherine yanked her door open and climbed in, slamming it shut. Rose and I continued down the street. Annie came out the side door of the restaurant with a bag of trash in her hand.

"Annie, do you know those men with Catherine? Kalen and Michael?"

"I haven't seen that other one before, but Kalen comes in sometimes. During our slow times, like around three or four, after the lunch crowd. Fact, he often meets up with that quiet guy who works in your building. You know the one I mean? The one who doesn't say much, but I think he has an accent."

"Carlos?"

"No. I think his name is Rick."

"Rico?"

"Yeah. Him. Funny thing, Rico gets a sandwich and a beer, but Kalen doesn't get anything. Just talks to Rico for a little while, pays the tab, and leaves. Leaves a big tip too."

"So they're friends?"

"I don't know. They never come in together or leave together. Kalen always leaves first and Rico leaves about five minutes later. Last time they were in, they had a big argument."

"Did you hear what it was about?"

Annie shook her head.

"Thanks, Annie." I thought about what she said. There was something about Kalen that just didn't fit. Maybe he was just an enigma.

Rose and I walked in silence for a block. Even the sun and fresh air didn't distract me from that scene in the parking lot.

"Except for that last thing, they were nice enough guys, I guess." I was thinking out loud.

"Yes, and it didn't go by me." Rose seemed unaffected by Catherine's row.

"What?"

"Laney Montgomery Carrington Daniels!" Rose only used my full name when she really wanted to get my attention. "What'dya mean 'What?' The fact that you kept glancing at Kalen all through lunch, unless your face was buried in your sandwich. Laney, he's too old for you."

"And you usually read me right, too, but not this time. I was trying to figure out if the guy was real or plastic." It was a mannequin industry joke, and Rose knew me well enough to laugh. I love Rose like a sister, but her loud, cackling laugh always caught me off guard.

"Yeah, he's smooth, but he's okay. Catherine's pretty tight with him, ya' know. He's always stopping by the shop to see her. Never stays very long, but he always asks how I'm doin' as he goes through to Catherine's workroom. He's sure got manners. His mama musta' done somethin' right." I was surprised Rose noticed, but mostly I wondered if his mother knew about his temper.

Murder Among the Mannequins

It was almost three o'clock when we got back to the mill. I pulled out my keys as Rose continued down the street.

"I need to check on Gran," Rose called over her shoulder, and disappeared into a neighboring rowhouse that she shared with the woman who raised her. She was protective of the petite but sturdy older woman, especially now while her brother and his kids were visiting. From a block away, I could hear Gran's voice.

"You kids git outside 'n play, y'hear?" I could tell she meant business. I could see where Rose got her fortitude. The door banged shut after the kids hit the sidewalk. I waved to the kids and continued on into the mill.

The parking lot seemed particularly empty, and the building quiet. The quiet was soothing, reminding me of the Sunday mornings I spent here as a child with Grandpa Albert. The building was a dilapidated old textile mill even then, thirty years from becoming the viable artists' colony it was today. Every time we entered the building, Grandpa Albert marched right in, never stopping to look up at the letters carved in the marble lintel above the door, but I did. The smooth, cold stone with deep cuts spelling out Hartmann Textiles. I loved the worn wooden floorboards and the old hauling elevator at the end of the hallway, with its manual rope pulley system that was used for moving raw goods and finished rolls of fabric to the loading door on the basement level. I spent many happy hours listening to Grandpa's stories of working for the imperious businessman William Hartmann, only to end up marrying his daughter, my Grandmother Emily.

Murder Among the Mannequins

I didn't need my key since someone had propped the mill's door open, in spite of the sign Elise had posted to keep the door locked. I frowned. There'd been several small things taken from the first floor studios in the past few weeks. Not enough to call the cops, but enough to be disconcerting. Even so, I appreciated not having to open it today. It was a heavy oak door that I usually had to put all my weight against to budge. I slipped inside and pulled the door shut firmly behind me.

Chapter 5

I managed to catch the elevator as the doors were closing. That was a good sign it was working today. I knew the old elevator took longer than the stairs, but it saved me from walking up a flight. Childish, I know, but that was my way of rebelling against my mother's concern about my weight.

With my keys still in my hand, I got out on the second floor and bumped into the security guard figure as I walked past the exhibit in the main corridor, in front of our studio. Instinctively, I caught and steadied the figure, putting my hand on his swinging key ring. This hallway display was Elise's idea, and I had finally quit arguing about it.

"Sorry, Chester." I was used to speaking to the figures. I'd grown up with them, after all, not unlike Candice Bergen with Charlie McCarthy.

I continued to the black door marked *Montgomery Mannequins* in gold script.

"I'm glad you're back," Elise said when I walked into the sunny office. I was immediately thrown back into work mode. "That client from Omaha has called twice. He wants to know when we'll ship the figures for his *Pioneers West* exhibit. When do you think the costumes will be done?" As project manager, costume researcher, figure dresser, and jack-of-all-trades at Montgomery Mannequins, I get to field most questions around the office. Elise's forte was promoting our product and schmoozing with clients, while mine was getting things out the door.

"I can finish them up next week, as soon as the hides come in. I'll call and tell him to hold his horses." I laughed and carried two books from my desk in the office into my tiny design room, "the cave." I immersed myself in reading about clothing of the eighteenth-century West, pulling various books off Albert's bookshelves. The research on the Suttler family would make sure we got all the details right for the Miss Prudence figure, the one with the great topaz brooch and antique satin dress. I wanted to finish my notes so I didn't have to face it in the morning. I needed to devote tomorrow exclusively to Rose's mannequin.

Elise knocked on my design room door, interrupting my thoughts. "Burl and I are leaving now. We'll lock the door behind us. You won't be long?"

"Wow, did I get sidetracked." A glance at my watch told me it was after five. "I'll just finish up this research and see you later at home."

"Remember, I'm cooking for you and Howard tonight. A new recipe. Six o'clock sharp," Elise said and walked out of the office. My mother had always been a good cook, but her dishes got even more delectable once she started taking classes at the Culinary Arts Institute a couple of years ago. That's how Howard came into our lives. Elise had met him in the introductory course, and they've been friends and classmates ever since. It wasn't until he came to Harbor Mill in search of studio space that we realized he was the one and only Howard Wills Decatur, an up and coming painter whose work was gaining popularity in a New York gallery. It was only after they started talking about opening a restaurant in Carter's Village that Howard agreed to show his paintings locally; the space would double as a gallery.

Howard struck me as a little squirrelly, but apparently Elise didn't see it, or didn't care. For someone who was planning to be a "silent partner," he was in Elise's kitchen a lot. I was beginning to get used to Howard being at our house often; he seemed to not mind being her sous-chef. They always did their testing in Elise's kitchen since Howard's apartment was built in the sixties and apparently had never been remodeled. He claimed he was waiting for his big score with his paintings in New York to get another place with a kitchen big enough for professional equipment. He seemed to be dragging his feet on that, but then why wouldn't he? Elise had a kitchen big enough for both of them. And he was always cleaning up as they cooked, a trait Elise appreciated. Me too, since it meant I wasn't called upon to help. I envied Elise's energy and her metabolism. And her willpower to just taste things, rather than gorge on those tasty morsels she prepared. I didn't have that same willpower.

It was dark by the time I gathered my things to leave the studio, but I felt accomplished. I pulled my collar close around my neck as I left the comfort of the old building. There were few cars left in the parking lot. I glanced up at the rising moon and noticed the beautiful, stark outlines of the bare trees. There was something comforting about the dark arriving early in the fall and winter. Like nature telling us it was time to stop working for the day. I was filled with thoughts of getting home to a fire in the fireplace and a good dinner.

It wasn't until I had turned onto Boston Street that I remembered I'd left Rose's dress upstairs. *Damn.* I debated with myself. If I made the few alterations tonight, I could have the figure ready on time tomorrow for the bridal show. I knew that having a doppelganger standing beside Rose was a sure way to get attention at the trade show. And more attention translated into more sales. Elise had proven that, once she began using her own double. I pouted when I thought again of her making a figure of me. Damn it, I really didn't want to take over the business. I was happy with the way things were.

Sighing, I turned around before getting on the highway, and hurried back to the mill. Clutching my coat around me rather than stopping to button it, I dug for my keys, trying not to count the seconds it took to retrace my steps. I didn't want to be late for dinner. The front door was slightly ajar, propped open with a rock. I'd really have to tell Elise to get after the tenants about this, even if they did have lots of boxes, bags, and paraphernalia to carry in and out.

The elevator's whirring and thumping resounded down the empty hall as I stepped out onto the second floor. The mill was rarely this quiet. The tenants were mainly artists who worked any time they could, nights and weekends especially. Tonight seemed to be one of the few nights the building itself seemed to be resting.

My key fit smoothly into the old lock, and in a minute I was inside Montgomery Mannequins. Using only the light from the streetlamps coming through the windows, I took the quickest route to the clean room, tracing Rose's steps earlier that day through the storage area. Rose was right about the hands. The arms and legs rested quietly against the wall, but the hands seemed to reach out. An involuntary shudder took me by surprise. I reached the door to the clean room and froze. A soft thud echoed from the far end of the room.

"Hello? Who's there?" I called, stepping backwards into the darkness of the storage area. There was no answer. I thought back quickly. Hadn't I locked the door when I left? Had Burl come back for something? I'd only been gone a few minutes.

I heard a shuffling noise. I ducked next door into my tiny design room and remained silent, trying not to breathe. With no windows, this room was pitch black. I didn't try to close the door; I knew the old hinges creaked. All I heard was silence. I slowly counted to one hundred, willing my heart to stop pounding. I listened carefully. Nothing. I decided I was being paranoid; I remembered locking the main door when I left. No one was in here but me. I gingerly poked my head out into the storage area and squinted into the darkness, then quietly made my way toward the light switch outside the office. Suddenly, two hands shot out of the darkness and I felt them around my throat. They were warm, not like the cold ones I was used to working with. I tried to scream, but only a strangled noise came out. I took a swing at my assailant, but I was knocked off-balance before my punch landed. I heard a thud the same time I felt it, and realized it was my head meeting the floor.

Chapter 6

*I*couldn't tell if the banging I was hearing was at the front door or inside my head. I fought my way back from darkness into consciousness and realized it was my head. I heard footsteps receding somewhere off in the distance and had a woozy picture of shoes floating around in my head. Groggily, I stood up and found the light switch, then stumbled to the front door and locked it. I leaned back against the heavy wooden door and breathed deeply to quiet my pounding heart, my hands shaking. Even with my eyes closed, I saw flashes of light. I slid to the floor to rest my shaking legs. I lifted a trembling hand and felt a lump of sore flesh rising on my forehead.

I opened my eyes slowly and, after a few moments, I got up, still leaning against the door. I felt a little steadier; the throbbing had subsided somewhat. I made my way into the same office that had been so bright and sunny just an hour ago. I forced myself to focus. *Dial 911*. The answering machine blinked at me from the desk. For a minute, I couldn't think what to do. I wanted to check the message and forget what had just happened.

I sat down in my desk chair gingerly and let my head clear for a moment. I dialed the police. I laughed when they put me on hold, and then grabbed my throbbing head. When someone finally came back on the line, there was so much background noise I was surprised he could hear me. I made my report brief, told him the intruder was gone, and hung up the phone. I neglected to mention I was conked on the head. I leaned back in the chair, now fully aware that I had to wait for the police to arrive. The clock on the answering machine said 5:27 p.m. I had to stop that damn blinking. I hit the play button.

"Sorry I missed you." I heard the familiar voice of Detective Dale Adams. He hesitated before speaking. "How about we go sailing again this weekend?" It sounded like he was anxious to move forward, which would please my mother no end, but I was happy right now with not having a commitment every weekend. Still, he was the kind of guy that you could check off everything in the pro column and nothing in the con column.

I chewed on my lip as I saved the message. "Damn," I said to the machine, "I'm not calling you back right now or I'll sound like a damsel in distress." I wasn't interested in another wounded-bird relationship. That's how it had started with Reggie. One flat tire had wasted eight years of my life.

I slowly got up from my chair. I felt a little steadier. The throbbing had subsided somewhat. I looked at my watch. It was 5:44 p.m. I walked toward the front door and stopped beside the figure of Grandpa Albert. I stared at the plaque: Albert Montgomery, Founder, Montgomery Mannequins. I never tired of looking at the accurate likeness, the details of his face. The figure looked just as I remembered him, with gentle crow's feet at the corners of his eyes, and just a hint of a dimple in his chin. He even had a five o'clock shadow of graying beard, as if it was the end of a long day.

"Well, Grandpa"—I patted the figure's shoulder—"It seems the police have forgotten about me. I guess I need to check around for any damage."

I felt shaky as I moved through the storage area. The eyeballs seemed to follow me, with the street lamps shining into the interior, glinting off the glass case. I hurried to the last of the four rooms, Burl's workshop, wanting to leave no space unchecked. The day's sawdust had been mostly swept up, but there were footprints disturbing the evenness of the broom marks. I couldn't tell if they were Burl's. All the bodies that were in progress and Burl's tools seemed to be in order.

I rubbed the back of my neck to soothe the creepy feeling that wouldn't go away. I entered the next room, where Burl did his vinyl casting. Burl had left the molds for tomorrow's firing lined up neatly on the prep table. I was glad that he insisted on propping open the black iron doors of the two large kilns with two by fours. The kilns were big enough to conceal a person. The idea of someone hiding in an oven made my nerves hum.

Next up the line was the clean room. It looked undisturbed. The two pioneer figures were lying on the large central worktable, just as I'd left them. In the back left corner, the Lafayette figure, complete with blue tailcoat, jewel-handled sword, and perfectly coiffed hair stood intact near the side door that opened directly into the office.

I inhaled sharply, which made me grab my throbbing head as I moved to the Miss Prudence figure in the front corner. This felt like a special job since I'd gotten to know Prudence in my research, and I hoped nothing had been damaged.

Miss Prudence stood just as I'd left her, in front of the photographer's backdrop paper waiting for her photo to be taken. She seemed to be intact. On the wall over her left shoulder hung the sepia photo loaned by my client to guide the job. Once again, I marveled at how closely Burl had captured the build and posture of the matronly Miss Prudence, and how exactly Rose had duplicated the dress, using a smoky-gold antique satin. Once the topaz pin that Catherine was still working on was in place, the figure would mimic the photo down to the last detail. Even the shoes were hand dyed and scuffed the way they were in the photograph.

"Oh no!" I said out loud. Behind Miss Prudence, the Rose figure lay on the ground, her arm lying sprawled two feet away.

"Oh no! Not the Rose!" I stood her upright and placed the arm on the worktable, after which I grabbed my head again to stop the throbbing. I'd inspect the arm socket and check for more damage tomorrow.

"Rose's dress!" Still holding my throbbing head, I realized what had brought me back into the mill in the first place. "I need to get it home," I said in more like a whisper. I'd left it hanging in the costume room, so I headed toward the back of the clean room, but then froze. I heard distant footsteps on the creaky wooden floor in the hallway outside the front door. The doorknob rattled. Had I locked it? My heart was now pounding more than my head. Surely my assailant wouldn't come back!

Chapter 7

I heard a knock. "Elise, Laney? Are you still here?" A familiar voice sounded muffled through the door.

"Howard!" I could have wished it was someone besides Howard, who was never good in a crisis, but even so, relief flooded through me. I hurried to the front and unbolted the door.

"What's wrong?" Howard stared at my face.

Howard was roughly my age, maybe a little younger, and not much taller. He was sporting his usual paint-covered smock—with his conservator's white cotton gloves peeking out of his pocket—over perfectly creased trousers. Standing eye to eye with him, I recited a very short version of what happened. "Someone knocked me out. Did you see any strangers in the building?"

"Knocked you out? In here? How did he get in? Are you all right?" He fired a stream of questions. Then in answer to mine, he said, "I haven't seen anyone, but I've been upstairs in my studio crating paintings to send out tomorrow. Are you okay?"

"I've got a nice bump on my head, but I'm more angry than scared." Angry at the nerve of the intruder. And angry at the police. "What time is it?"

"Five fifty-five."

"Thirty minutes! It feels like it's been hours. Where are the police?"

"You're shaking, Laney. Sit down." He led me to the small reception area up front, just inside the front door. It was the one comfortable area in the studio, the first place guests were ushered, and a far cry from the wall of body parts that once greeted Grandpa Albert's clients.

"Howard, I didn't know anyone was still here." I slid stiffly into a green, overstuffed chair and watched him turn on the table lamp in the corner. "Thank God you're in town. What brought you down here so late?"

Howard waved a piece of paper. "I was going to tape a note to your door. I need Elise to let the freight driver into my studio tomorrow. My paintings are being picked up at ten, and I have a nine o'clock class at MICA and a conference call with New York at ten thirty."

"I'm sure that's no problem," I agreed, massaging my temples. Howard was very protective of his studio and its contents; Elise was the only person he trusted with a key, and even that was a concession on his part. She insisted on having a master to all the offices and studios. I leaned back against the soft Naugahyde.

"Are they going to your new gallery in New York?" Always the perfectionist, Howard had removed his paintings from three galleries in the last two years because he didn't feel they were getting the proper exposure. "Is there such a thing as the perfect gallery?" I knew I'd said the wrong thing when Howard bit on his upper lip. Chalking his sensitivity up to his artist's personality, I quickly placated him. "I'd like to see one of your gallery shows sometime." I knew I'd have a better chance of seeing his work out in a gallery, even if it meant going to New York or waiting till the restaurant opened, than inside his studio on the third floor.

"Actually, I've finally talked Elise into coming to New York in a few weeks. You know how I value her opinion." I think he enjoyed the maternal attention my mother gave him, and I can't say I minded her having someone else to focus on besides me.

I looked at Howard and shouted, "Oh my God, Elise's dinner!" as we both jumped up. My head pounded again.

"Oh, jeez, I'd forgotten it was tonight! She wouldn't let me help prepare this one. Thank heavens you remembered, Laney. She would never have forgiven me if I missed it."

"We're going to be late, Howard. Even if we leave now." I checked my watch. It was 6:05 p.m.

"How long have you been waiting for the cops?"

"Too long."

"Anything taken?"

"I don't think so. But whoever it was knocked over one of the mannequins. I'll need to do some repairs on it tomorrow. I didn't check the costume room yet; that's when you scared the daylights out of me. Wait a minute, will you, while I go get Rose's dress?"

I poked my head in the costume room, draped the garment bag with Rose's dress over my arm, and emerged. "I don't think anything was disturbed in there. Ready to go, Howard?" I didn't want to admit I was glad he'd be following me to my car.

"Yes, but drive slowly this time."

I laughed, risking another headache. My fast driving was a habit left over from earlier days. I hadn't exactly had a stellar driving record in my "growing up years," as Elise happily related to everyone who knew me. Even now, everyone teased me about driving my old Honda Civic as if it were a sports car.

Gingerly rubbing the knot on my head, I gathered my jacket and bag from the office. I glanced at the phone and thought again of Dale. *I couldn't handle one more thing tonight*, I thought as I closed the door. I climbed into the front seat of my car and tossed the garment bag on the passenger seat. I leaned back and closed my eyes to let the dizziness pass. The events of the last hour were still running through my head like a movie.

The drive from East Baltimore to Carter's Village took only twenty minutes. Howard had no trouble following me at this time of evening, but even with an unwitting bodyguard, I checked for any headlights that followed us for too long. We just missed the knot of commuters hurrying home. Even at rush hour, the streets were always quiet once I turned off the highway toward Carter's Village. I slowed to a crawl, enjoying the lights twinkling in the windows of the old Victorian houses and feeling my breathing slow. The heart of the village—Chesapeake Bank, Lyons' grocery, the post office, and the library—were all dark now. The village clock and the old-time gaslight, now electrified, marked my turn onto Hartmann Avenue. I didn't miss the old rutted lane that was eventually paved and named for my great-grandfather. Those ruts hadn't prevented me from catching the school bus on rainy days, but they had delivered me in muddy shoes.

I loved the approach down Hartmann Avenue to our house, RoseHaven. It made me think of my great-grandfather, William Hartmann, who had purchased nearly fifty acres of wooded land with a great Victorian house, an old manor house, and a barn. He had a large space cleared for a rose garden for my great-grandmother. Our rose garden was still the highlight of the Carter's Village Garden Tour each year, though it was becoming a thorn in Elise's side, and mine. It was a given that with ownership of RoseHaven came the responsibility of keeping up the heirloom roses.

I pulled straight back to the side of the house, leaving the space in the front circular drive free for Howard. I walked across to the front door and let Howard in. Jesse, my chocolate Labrador retriever, came running up to meet us, jumping up with both paws on Howard's chest. She stood nearly as tall as Howard and weighed nearly as much.

"Get down, Jesse." I pushed the dog down. "Hi, Mom, we're here. Sorry we're late," I called, hoping she wouldn't make a scene with Howard standing there. I scratched Jesse's ears.

"Good. You can set the table," Elise's voice came from the dining room.

I shrugged off my coat and tossed it at the hall tree in the oak-paneled foyer, catching it on a hook. Howard walked to the closet and hung his jacket and scarf on a hanger, buttoning the first button and brushing a leaf from the lapel. I chuckled at the thought that he might have used a lint roller, had one been handy.

"I need a minute to hang up Rose's dress," I called to Elise, grabbing my head to ease the throbbing. Turning to Howard, I lowered my voice. "Keep her entertained, Howard."

I slipped back through the butler's pantry, into the kitchen. Off to the right was the large room that served as my quarters. Jesse followed on my heels. I hung Rose's dress on the back of the bedroom door, closing it at the same time. Stepping into the bathroom, I gulped down a couple of aspirin and looked in the mirror. I ran my fingers through my hair, thankful for once for the unruly curls that covered the lump on my head and the frown lines on my forehead. Back in my bedroom, I unzipped Rose's garment bag and laid her dress carefully across the foot of the bed. It really was a beauty. The simple lines and subtle, curving décolletage made it a stunning dress, a surefire seller for Rose.

"Laney, where are you?" came Elise's voice.

I grabbed my linen blazer from the back of the overstuffed chair, gave it a shake, and threw it on over my blouse. I grabbed a silk scarf and hurried out to the dining room. Already I was beginning to feel better, and decided to put off telling Elise about the attack until after dinner.

Howard was filling Elise in on the freight pickup tomorrow. I caught his eye and made a shushing motion with my finger, signaling to him to keep quiet about the break-in.

Chapter 8

"You look nice, dear." Elise looked up from folding the napkins. She insisted on a formal setting, a sort of coming out party for the food when she was close to a final recipe. I had to agree that presentation went a long way. I didn't mind this angle of her retirement plans.

"I'll get the wine." I took three wine glasses and three water goblets from the cabinet. At the kitchen counter I poured Merlot, admiring its ruby color and fragrant aroma, and handed the wine glasses to Howard and Elise, who were now standing over the stove admiring the browned goose. Elise lifted the goose onto a serving platter while Howard wiped up the drips. I filled the remaining goblets with ice water and carried them into the dining room, setting them at the tip of the knives. I chuckled to myself. Being a doctor's wife for eight years had come in handy after all. The sum of my life during that time was that I could set a formal table blindfolded. I also learned that I hated cooking. *Maybe their restaurant isn't such a bad idea after all.* I didn't know if that was a comforting thought or a threatening one.

Crash! A loud noise came from the back of the house, from the direction of the garage, making me jump. Jesse growled and raced to the back door with her hackles up. We rushed to look outside, me to the kitchen door and Elise to the window above the kitchen sink. I saw nothing except darkness and shadows. Had my attacker followed me home? More angry than scared, I flipped on the outside light, flooding much of the backyard with brightness. Opening the door, we both stepped outside. Angry as I was, I was still glad to know Elise had my back. Literally. And knowing Howard was inside and could call for help was a comforting third-tier backup.

"It's only me, Mrs. Carrington," called a voice from the shadow of the garage.

"Ted? Is that you?" Elise peered into the shadows.

Ted emerged into the light. "I'm sorry," he said, dropping both his voice and his eyes. "I was just leaving the extra bags of mulch for tomorrow. I saw you had company and I was trying not to disturb you. Looks like I didn't manage it. I tripped over the paint cans by the garage door." He looked sheepish.

"Come inside, your elbow is bleeding," insisted Elise.

"It'll be okay. I'll just see you in the morning."

"First come in and get a bandage," I directed. "You're dripping blood all over the sidewalk."

Ted looked down, then stepped inside, and took the towel I handed him. He looked trim and tan from the summer's work. I hadn't been able to pinpoint his age when we'd hired him, and he had matured considerably in the year he had worked for us, tending the heirloom rose garden. He was quite good at gardening, in fact. He's the one who kept RoseHaven on the Garden tour. My great-grandmother would be very happy knowing we'd carried on her tradition, even if we did have to pay someone to do it. She had spent many hours tending and nurturing her roses. It was important to her to keep the heirloom strains alive. As a child, I had loved to play outside and take in their deep, full-bodied scents. Elise had not tended to them as much as her grandmother had, and the garden had fallen into a scruffy existence before we found Ted. I'd thought he was maybe thirty-five and was surprised to learn after we hired him that he was in his midtwenties. He had a self-contained, worldly air about him, as though he had been on his own for quite a few years. He held up his bleeding arm, which was covered with a fine layer of light brown hair, lighter than his dark locks and day-old beard. It was the first time I had been this close to him. Part of a tattoo was peeking out from the short sleeve of his T-shirt. Was it a wing? No, it looked like an eagle. No, an angel, or was it a lion's mane, or part of a mythical beast?

"I can't believe you're only wearing a T-shirt, Ted. Aren't you cold?" He just smiled.

Ted had been a loner ever since I'd known him. I would occasionally see him around the shops in Carter's Village. He was always alone. He usually stopped in at RoseHaven once a week to see what needed to be done. He had been reluctant to leave a phone number, but finally did at Elise's insistence. The one time I had to call him, I heard plenty of background noise. Was it a party? Roommates? A bar? The TV? I suspected one of the last two.

"Hey, Ted, I could use some help moving things out of my studio. You available next week?" Howard called from behind us.

Elise spoke up. "After the roses. We've got dibs on him right now, Howard."

"Sure, sure, once I take care of Mrs. Carrington's roses." Ted avoided Elise's gaze. I realized this time it was a combination of pride and embarrassment. That's why I liked Ted. He was a simple man. He didn't need much in life; he seemed to be content to garden and tend to odd jobs of caretaking. He loved dirt under his fingernails, and he didn't mind hard work.

"Well, it's good you know so much about roses. Elise would be lost without you."

Elise shot Howard a "thanks a lot" look, and then admitted, "It's true, ever since our roses became the highlight of the Carter's Village Garden Club's annual tour. I certainly can't keep up with all those bushes. And, since it was disclosed that some of them are antique roses, the Garden Club would never allow us to *not* take care of them."

I smiled, "If Great-Grandmother Elisabeth could see all the fuss over her roses! She'd be pleased that others were enjoying them as much as she did."

Ted took the bandage I offered him. "Well, you gotta love your work, I always say."

"I heartily agree," I said. "Howard could never do anything but paint, right, Howard?" I looked over to see Howard tidying up crumbs off the counter.

"Right. Even if I won the lottery. I might be painting in Tahiti, but I would still be painting." He threw the crumbs into the sink and rinsed them down.

"For me it's cooking and mannequins—what a combination." Elise laughed while she arranged the goose on a huge mound of wild rice on its enormous platter. "But I have enjoyed it!"

"'You 'gotta love your work' is right, Ted." I laughed as old memories came flooding back. "One Halloween we brought Albert Einstein home and stood him inside the front door. Scared the daylights out of the kids! And once we dressed Elise's figure in a sarong at the office, so we wouldn't miss her while she was on a trip to Hawaii." I looked at Elise. "And remember when we gathered all the old keys we could find and hung them on Chester's key ring? Wow, it must be two years since we dressed that security guard figure."

Elise looked puzzled for a moment, but then nodded.

Ted moved to the door. "Sorry to disturb your dinner, Mrs. Carrington."

"Why don't you stay, Ted? We certainly have enough."

"No thanks, I gotta get home." Then looking from Elise to me, he said, "I'll be back tomorrow afternoon to put your roses to bed." Ted was careful not to let the door slam. I watched out the back door as he disappeared around the corner of the house, and wondered where home was.

I followed Howard and Elise into the dining room as she set the platter on the table. "Oh! It looks perfect," Howard gushed, and I had to agree. We sat down in silence. Elise watched us intently as we sampled the goose.

"Mom, you've done it." I sat back in my chair. "It tastes even better than it smells. I don't know how, but you've solved the challenge you were having with the gamey flavor." Goose wasn't my favorite meat, but she had worked her magic and it was pretty good.

Elise said one word, "Fennel."

"Perfect," Howard said, savoring a mouthful.

Elise picked up her fork and began to eat. "How come you were so late?"

Oh great! I knew I couldn't avoid telling her forever, so I took a breath and plunged right in.

"Well, I wanted to wait until after dinner, but . . . I need to tell you that we had an intruder at the shop."

Elise stopped in midbite.

I hurried to explain. "I had already left the office, but when I went back up for Rose's dress, I heard a noise and then, well, he hit me. He or she," I added.

"Laney, my God, why didn't you call me?" Elise put down her fork. I didn't know if she was concerned for my welfare or the shop's.

"Because I only blacked out for a few moments. Howard came down to leave a note on our door, and I had already come to."

"You blacked out? You were unconscious? Let me see your eyes. We have to get you to the doctor." She stood up.

"I'm fine." I waved her concern away. "And I checked everything in the office. The only thing that was damaged was the Rose figure, and I can fix her tomorrow." I answered my mother's one unasked question. "Nothing was touched, not the computers, not even the petty cash in the desk drawer. I called the police, but when they didn't show up after half an hour, I left. That's why I'm late."

"Well, stop by the police station tomorrow on your way to work and file a report. Maybe your friend Dale will be in." The way she said "your friend" had that motherly overtone that still made me cringe.

"Dale's in homicide, Mom. He won't take the report." I skirted the real subject. She took every opportunity to throw us together. She still thought I needed a man. I was perfectly happy with my life the way it was. I really needed to get my own place.

Elise gave her predictable answer. "Well, go anyway. And then go have yourself checked out, if you're not going to go tonight." Living back home with my mother was beginning to be a pain.

I left Elise and Howard at the table discussing the finer points of seasoning fowl and carried my dishes to the dishwasher. That was as close as I came to housework. Out of sight, out of mind, was my motto. I went into the living room and flipped on the nightly news. Fifteen minutes into it, I had heard about one murder-suicide, two suspicious fires, and a jewelry heist in Roland Park. I flipped the TV off, vowing not to watch the news ever again until they started reporting a balanced view of life in Baltimore, not just the crime stats and political bickering.

I tucked the *Baltimore Sun* under my arm and headed back to my quarters. I guess it was a pretty good setup if you had to live at home. It was more than a room and less than an apartment, so I thought of it as my "quarters." Grandpa Albert had added this room off to the right side of the kitchen at the back of the house, which served as a playroom when Elise was young. Measuring fourteen by twenty feet, it included a full bath. It had a huge walk-in closet, which I converted from a toy closet. The room had a door which led out to the rose garden in the backyard, which Jesse thought of as her own private entrance. Jesse was waiting patiently there, only lightly pawing the paint off the doorframe, so I let her out for her nightly romp. She galumphed off across the yard and into the woods, her rich brown coat gleaming in the moonlight.

Tossing the newspaper on the bed, I settled down in the wing chair and pulled Rose's dress onto my lap. I reached to remove the purple iolite pin that Catherine had made specifically for this gown, remembering how nicely it fit at the point of the V-neck of the bodice. I gasped. There was no pin! I jumped up and searched around the chair legs, then near the door and under the bed. No pin anywhere. I thought hard; I didn't remember taking the pin off the dress at the studio. But I must have. Where else could it be? It was the first thing I'd look for tomorrow. Catherine wouldn't have time to make a new one.

Frowning, I sat back down and made the alterations to the waistline of Rose's dress by hand. When I finished, I hung the dress on the back of the door, and realized I'd need to use the professional steamer at the studio tomorrow to finish it up.

Murder Among the Mannequins

I let out a sigh and stretched. What a day! I walked to the back door and looked out at the moonlight on the roses. There were a few blooms left. Ted really did a nice job with them, year-round. Jesse was already waiting to come in and immediately placed her cold nose in my hand and shook off the chill when she came inside.

I locked the door and headed for a warm shower. I slipped into a soft T-shirt, and then climbed into bed with the newspaper. A robbery in Guilford, a fire in East Baltimore, and a declining Dow. Great! It was as bad as the television news. I yawned and turned out the light; I'd better be well rested, for tomorrow was the deadline, and a tight one at that, for Rose's mannequin. But my thoughts wouldn't stop. I gingerly felt the knot on my head. It reminded me I had to squeeze in a visit to the police station and the doctor's office. What could the intruder have been looking for? The office equipment and what little cash we kept in a drawer weren't touched. It looked like he—I assumed it was a he, since it was someone taller and stronger than me—had barreled through the clean room like a tornado. But why? And where was Rose's pin? Why would someone want it enough to break in? Oh, and then there was Dale....

Chapter 9

*M*mm, mmm, bacon and eggs! I smelled it before I opened my eyes and tried to ignore the delicious aroma as I slipped into a pair of jeans. I could pinch the waistband in an inch. The battle was relentless, but it finally felt like I was making headway.

"Gone are the days of eating whatever we want." I scratched Jesse's long, floppy ears. "Guess it's the same with your senior diet." Jesse looked up at me and tucked her nose back into the warm circle of dark brown fur. The events of last night came flooding back. Including that I should return Dale's call. I supposed I should tell him what happened at the mill before he heard it through the blue grapevine.

Jesse leapt off the bed and stood at the window, watching a squirrel race across the backyard. She let out a high-pitched whine.

"Wait a minute!" It came out more sharply than I intended. The soft tapping of Jesse's nails as she paced at the door broke my resolve.

"All right, all right, I can take a hint." I donned my oatmeal-colored sweater and picked up a lightweight cotton jacket. It was good that Jesse made me get some exercise.

The parcel was an odd-shaped lot, much smaller than the forty-seven acres that my great-grandfather had bought in 1915. Now down to five acres, the property was still large by suburban standards.

Murder Among the Mannequins

Jesse took off on her usual morning route, out to the front of the property close to Hartmann Road. I stood on the driveway between the house and my car, waiting for her usual routine: a sharp U-turn at the front point of property, then running back around the house past me at breakneck speed, past the falling remains of the original manor house, past the carriage house and the barn, and then disappearing into the woods. She was heading down the old driveway, an overgrown dirt lane that snaked back through the woods and encircled the property. I followed, brushing away the overhanging pine branches, not even trying to keep up with her. Her route didn't vary much unless she spotted a squirrel or fox. The dirt lane emerged from the woods, completing the circle five hundred feet down Hartmann Road, around a curve that put it out of sight of the paved drive to the house. Only old-timers knew that the two woods-shrouded driveways were connected. I caught up with Jesse at the end of the wooded drive. I could see she was sniffing around a person standing at the edge of Hartmann Road. As I got closer, I saw it was Ansel, the old guy whom I often spotted walking around Carter's Village. I knew he carried dog treats in his pocket and was sure that's what attracted Jesse. He waved a small greeting and kept on his rounds up Hartmann Rd toward the village. I petted Jesse as I watched Ansel shuffling along in his worn shoes. I didn't know Ansel very well since he never stopped long enough to speak to me. He struck me as a little odd, so I was happy to keep my distance.

Jesse made a U-turn and circled back toward the house. Her last stop was the rose garden just behind the kitchen. It always amused me that she routinely left the house through the door in my quarters, yet returned to the kitchen door, even though the two were only twelve feet apart along the back of the house. I guess she knew where the food was. When I caught up to her, I smelled bacon again as soon as I opened the door.

"Wipe those feet," Elise mumbled between bites of her high calorie, high protein breakfast. "And paws," she called, reaching for the jelly. I didn't know how she could eat like that and still stay so thin. Unfortunately, I took after my father, who was always portly.

"I wish I'd added a mudroom outside the kitchen when I had the other renovations done," Elise mentioned for the umpteenth time. I snagged a paper towel from the counter and wiped Jesse's paws while she sat patiently. The dog, too, knew the drill.

Jesse picked up her bowl in her teeth and ran over to Elise, tail wagging, saliva flowing.

"I know. Your mother is running late, as always. Just let me finish this article, Jesse." I always cringed at her calling me Jesse's mother, but I had lost that battle too. Jesse sat down beside Elise, the bowl still clenched in her teeth.

I had to smile at my mother. A confirmed cat lover, Elise had begrudgingly agreed to allow a dog in the house. Now, three years later, not only did Elise talk to Jesse, but Jesse listened.

Putting down her newspaper, Elise asked, "How's your head this morning?" Before I could answer, she instructed, "I think you should see Dr. Park."

"I'm fine. I took something for the headache. I'll be okay." I took the bowl out of Jesse's mouth and filled it with dry food, since I knew from experience that Elise would be absorbed with the newspaper for a while. Jesse followed at my heels, jumping up and down.

"You'll always be a puppy at heart, won't you, Jesse?" I said, taking her face in both hands. Jesse gobbled the contents of the bowl in thirty seconds. Ears crinkled, she walked back to Elise and slid down on the floor, waiting for the dry food to slide into her stomach. I put a bowl of fresh water down and poured a cup of coffee. "Great coffee, Mom. It's a new blend, isn't it?" I wasn't as much of a coffee gourmand as she was, but I could tell a good cup from a bad cup, even with the cream and sugar I added. Elise thought I was disguising the flavor, but I was really making it palatable.

"Yes. I thought I knew all the brands at the River House Café, but I discovered their Virgin Brazilian Roast just yesterday. It's proprietary; they roast it on the premises. When I asked for details, a new server reluctantly pulled out the notes on the beans and read them to me."

"She probably thought you were a Java spy, gathering information for your restaurant-to-be."

Elise put down her paper and looked at me with resignation on her face. She breathed deeply and there was a long pause. "I've put a contract on the old pharmacy building on Chandler Street."

"What?" I had heard her, but I couldn't believe it.

"I told you I was serious about this."

"But you said you were going to use the old barn on our property." It sounded whiney, even to me. I had harbored vague hopes that this restaurant would be a part-time endeavor, and she wouldn't have to retire from Montgomery Mannequins. Buying a building made her retirement more real.

"Too much renovation. And way too far from the Village. Howard and I will need the foot traffic in town to get started." When did the restaurant become "Howard's and mine"? Chandler Street was right in the heart of Carter's Village. It was, in fact, the first street that had ever been paved in the town, and therefore became the shopping district. It's true the retail spaces were small by today's commercial standards, but the buildings had much more character, and were in great demand; they were never empty for long. The pharmacy building was larger than the other Victorian-era storefronts, having been added onto in the 1950s.

"With all the space here and all the old buildings, it's a shame you had to buy more property." I didn't know what difference it made, except that this made her decision concrete. It meant she'd have to run the restaurant full time.

Elise raised her right eyebrow like she did when I was a kid.

"All right. No more arguing about the restaurant. But the mannequin business is another matter. I've loved it, but I'm ready to retire and do something else. It's time to pass the torch."

I grumbled to myself, but said nothing. *No sense rehashing that conversation.* Elise returned to burying herself in her newspaper, and I grabbed my coffee cup and retreated to my quarters.

I needed to busy myself with something. I took Rose's dress from the hook on my bedroom door, put it into the garment bag, and headed back through the kitchen.

"I have to get Rose's figure repaired and delivered today. Her bridal show is tomorrow at the Redwood Hotel. She's staying there tonight since her brother and his kids are in town staying with Gran. Those kids have taken over the house. How does your day look?"

"Busy. I'll stop in the office, but then I need to meet with our accountant. After that, I'm picking up the Massachusetts clients at the airport at noon and taking them to lunch at the Inner Harbor. We'll be going over their blueprints and exhibit designs to see where they want to put figures. Will you be in later, in case we get as far as discussing costumes?"

"I'll be working on Rose's mannequin this morning, but I can't make any promises about being in after lunch. I need to deliver Rose's figure to the hotel before five o'clock. Tell the clients I'll be in touch about the costumes. I'd better get going before I start chopping potatoes and onions to fry in that bacon grease."

I poured a second cup of coffee and picked up Rose's dress, my car keys, and my jacket. I hated making several trips to the car, preferring instead to juggle three or four things at one time and take fewer steps, except of course, the ones needed to retrieve what I inevitably would drop.

Elise was buried in the newspaper. "Listen to this, Laney, 'Upscale Area Burglarized. Police are searching to find a connection between three break-ins in the Guilford-Roland Park area of Baltimore.' And look at this picture of the necklaces and rings that were stolen! Look at the size of those stones. Wow!"

"Hmm." I looked over her shoulder. "Which reminds me. I need to stop by the police station and give them a report about the break-in. I'm not looking forward to that."

"Laney, those officers have more to do than worry about you not waiting for them last night," Elise chided.

I knew it was not "those officers," but one in particular who was making me procrastinate this morning. I hadn't returned Dale's call last night. As a homicide detective, he worked out of Headquarters, not the South Baltimore precinct, but by now he might have heard about the break-in "over the wire" as they said. The local guys knew he had a thing for me. I was pretty sure he would be there, and I wasn't in the mood for a public lecture. I went into my room, put everything but the coffee mug down on the bed, and picked up the phone. He'd be less angry if he heard it from me, and I really did owe him an explanation.

It was a short conversation that ended with an order. "What the hell were you thinking, Laney? Meet me at the station in twenty minutes!"

Chapter 10

*T*wenty minutes later, I nosed into a visitor's parking spot in front of the Southeast Police Station. I fumbled in my purse for my elusive hairbrush.

"Damn," I said out loud and resorted to running my hands through my hair. *Good enough.*

"Damn," I said again. One kiss had changed everything. Before last weekend, I would have walked right in the front door and asked if my friend, "The Professor," as the younger guys called fifty-year-old Dale Adams, was here. But instead here I was, glued to the car seat, feeling...I don't know what I was feeling. I think it was dread. Dale was a nice guy. It just seemed that everyone but me was pushing this relationship. I had already donated eight years of my life to someone else before I took it back, and I liked my life just fine now. Ten years ago, I married Reggie Daniels, a med student, after a whirlwind courtship. I survived his resident year, which was pretty much like not being married, and moving to Pennsylvania, and seven more years of social climbing. It took me that long to realize I didn't want that one-dimensional life. Then when Elise broke her leg and fractured her wrist stepping off a curb, it was the prompt I needed to change my life. I moved home to help her run the house and the business. I exchanged one plastic life for another, I jokingly thought.

A tap on the back window of the car caused me to jump. I knew who it was before I turned around. I moved quickly, jumping out and closing the car door before Dale was beside me.

"Hey."

"Hey yourself." I gave him my best casual grin.

"I saw you sitting in the car. You okay?"

"Yeah."

"You didn't make the guys happy, leaving the scene last night."

"Yeah, well, if they hadn't taken their sweet time, they would have found me there." I thought he had a lot of nerve, blaming me for the uniforms' poor response time.

"Yeah, I guess it did take them a while." Dale shook his head. He knew the BCPD had a reputation for lousy response times. Unless a body was involved.

There was a silence, but I could tell he was more concerned than angry.

"Come on, let's go in. I made the boys promise to leave their guns strapped down."

"Ha ha," I said without mirth, but I caught his softened gray-blue eyes.

Up until Saturday, I'd been comfortable with him. I liked him, I really did. We could be silly and casual, just the way I wanted to keep things. His crooked smile appeared, making me feel comfortable again.

"Hold your fire, guys," Dale joked as he gently guided me in front of him into the old red-brick building that had once been a hardware store. The original planks of pine floorboards were wide and uneven. They creaked and groaned from years of suspects, officers, and visitors shuffling up and down the hallways. The place was noisy and chaotic.

"I've apprehended our fugitive," Dale called across the lobby to Sergeant Arnie Driscoll, who was sitting at the front desk.

Arnie ran his hand through what was left of his graying hair. I'd known him, too, since I was a kid. He grew up a block from the mill. Grandpa Albert had told me stories of Arnie loitering around the mill, pestering Grandpa into a part-time job when he was in high school. I guess plastic body parts couldn't compete with the lure of the real thing, so he had applied to the police academy after high school.

I waved and greeted Arnie. "How many days left now?"

"Forty-two. But who's counting?" He laughed, and then added, "We're already planning the party and you're invited."

"Good. Then maybe you'll come work for us when you retire." I smiled.

"Security?" Dale's brow furrowed. "I hate to be the one to break it to you, but the department doesn't get too many calls for stolen body parts." He chuckled. "Criminals aren't interested in arts and crafts. They sure aren't interested in your inventory."

"Well, someone was interested last night," I snapped. *Shit!* Sometimes Dale could be oblivious. Arnie just shook his head and picked up the ringing phone.

Dale didn't say anything, just steered me down the hall leading away from the front desk and into a room full of officers and desks and ringing phones.

He leaned in and whispered, "I want to talk to you before you leave. I'll be in the break room." I took a seat at the desk of the officer who waved me over.

It only took a few minutes to give the details as he madly scribbled his report. I was surprised how short the report was. Just a few pertinent questions: when and where, but no who, how, and certainly no why.

When he asked for a description, all I could give him was "strong hands" and "taller than me." As I left the room and headed toward the front door of the station, Dale came up behind me and caught my elbow. He led me into the break room. Two cops inside picked up their coffee cups, shot Dale a sly look, and left the room. It was the same look my mother gets when she mentions Dale's name.

"You know, the other guys wouldn't tell you this, and maybe I shouldn't, but there have been a rash of break-ins in the area. I'm really glad you weren't hurt. Thank God you weren't." He stopped short. "You weren't, were you?" I laughed at his sudden "aha" moment.

"Not really, short of a bump on the head, but it's nice to be asked."

Dale was quiet for a moment. "I wondered why you didn't call me last night."

"After I got home, Mom was fixing one of her new dishes. You know how she likes to test them on me. And then I had to alter Rose's dress. It just got too late to call." I knew I was rambling. He reached for my hand, but I drew it away, conveniently finding a loose thread on my jacket to rescue. He hesitated before saying, "How about another sail? Or a movie? Dinner?" His eyebrows shot up, making him look hopeful.

I knew he loved sailing. "Maybe a sail. I promise I'll call you, Dale," I put him off. "But right now, I want to get to the doctor."

"I thought you said you were all right," Dale said, following so closely behind that if I stopped suddenly, his gun would have made an impression on my backside.

"I am. But I promised Elise I'd go. Forget about it, I'm fine." I tried to sound casual.

He shook his head. "Elise. Always the businesswoman. Probably wants a record if there's an insurance claim in the future."

I stopped and abruptly turned to him. "Hey!" I said sharply. Arnie turned to look at us, and I lowered my voice. "You don't have to get into our family conflicts. I'll work it out." I was filled with conflicting emotions: concern for Dale's feelings, and annoyance at what I heard as his verbal attack on Elise and feeling the need to defend her. But I knew he was right. She was the businesswoman, not me.

I left the police station feeling worse than when I came in.

Chapter 11

I drove the two blocks to the walk-in clinic. I hated wasting time walking, and now that I had committed to see a doctor, I had to follow through, if only for a follow-up report to those who were so interested in the details of my life.

I was out in a record twenty minutes. Aside from a nagging headache, I didn't have any other symptoms. Dr. Park checked my eyes for signs of a concussion and handed me a prescription for a painkiller, which I promptly pocketed. I had no time to be groggy. I'd take some aspirin when I got to my desk.

I dodged through the rush-hour traffic to cross the street and duck into Annie's. Only the locals knew they served breakfast. They didn't advertise; in fact their sign said simply Lunch and Dinner Served. I headed for the cappuccino machine they had recently added while I waited for my bacon and egg sandwich to be ready. It would have been cheaper and faster eating at home, but I wanted to avoid Elise's nagging. Plus, I figured the calories wouldn't count if Elise didn't see me eating this stuff. I told myself it was because I wanted to support Annie's, which was also true. Annie was busy in the back, so I waved and made a quick exit.

I pulled into the mill's half-full parking lot and silently thanked Elise for posting Reserved signs on two spots for us. I gobbled down the rest of my breakfast before wiping my hands on my jeans, grabbing Rose's garment bag, and heading toward the front door. I held the heavy doors open for Rico, who had pulled into the parking lot behind me. I called a greeting to him, but he just nodded and avoided my eyes while going down the hall toward his studio door. He had been a tenant for a year, but always kept to himself. He had chosen the studio at the end of the hall.

"Be careful," I called as he went down the hall. The lighting was dim to nonexistent at the end of the hall. The only thing past his studio was the very old, very unused freight elevator, designed for hauling bolts of textiles to the basement in Great-Grandfather's day. On most floors, this was a good spot for the artists to store their unused canvases, since no one used this elevator any more.

Upstairs, I let myself in through the black door with the gold script, dropped my jacket on my chair, and glanced through the morning mail. Most of it was for Elise and could wait until later. I popped two Tylenol™ tablets and called a greeting to Burl, whose deep, melodious voice wafted up to the office from his workshop. He often sang when he was alone. It was a comforting sound, especially this morning; I hoped he wouldn't stop once he realized I was there.

I carried Rose's dress into the clean room and swept my hand across the table, making a clean spot to lay it down. Something shiny went skittering across the table. It was Rose's iolite pin! I was sure I didn't take it off the dress last night, although . . . it would have made sense to take it off and leave it at work . . . I stopped, savoring the quiet, and thought about the strange happenings of last night. It was weird. Nothing seemed to be stolen or disturbed, other than the Rose figure being damaged. The police didn't seem concerned enough to send someone to investigate. My glance rested on the far end of the worktable. I noticed I had left power tools out overnight, and hadn't swept up.

"Damn," I blurted out loud. "I forgot to mention the footprints in the sawdust for the police report." I walked out through the storage area and poked my head into Burl's workshop. The sawdust was still there, although the prints were now compromised by Burl's.

"Burl, don't walk through this sawdust anymore until I can call the police."

He looked at me with a quizzical look, and I remembered he knew nothing of last night.

"Someone broke in last night and had an altercation with me," I told him as I pushed my bangs aside and showed him the lump on my head.

"Jeez, Laney. Thank goodness you weren't hurt worse. You could have been killed! Who was it, did you see?"

I shook my head and asked, "Have you noticed if anything's missing?" I hadn't noticed anything last night, but I knew Burl would know in an instant if one of his tools was out of place.

He looked around carefully. "There's nothing missing, but I did think it was odd that sawdust was in the walkway. I always at least sweep it into a pile." He gestured to the corner, where a pile of sawdust lay but had been kicked or walked through.

"Thanks for reminding me, Burl. I need to report this." After I dialed the precinct's non-emergency number and told them about the footprints that might be of interest, they assured me there'd be someone by today, and cautioned us about obliterating them.

I pulled a chair over to protect the potential evidence. *This might be a good time to feel Burl out regarding my idea.* I pulled over a second chair and sat down.

"Burl, have you thought any more about buying out Elise? You have your heart in this company." He remained silent and continued working. Finally, he turned and laid down his tools.

"I don't think I'm the one to run your company. I just want to sculpt, and build your figures. You and Elise are much better at the office details. And the customers." It was clear he already thought of it as my company.

My heart sank. I was hoping he'd be my ace in the hole, but I realized I was trying to plug him into a hole he didn't want to fit into. *Join the club*, I thought.

"Well, just think about it," I persisted. "I'd still be around for consultation. You know the QuiltArts studio is just below us on the first floor, and I really want to spend more time there."

I left him and went back to the clean room. I took the tools off the table and put them away, and used a soft brush to clean off the remaining sawdust. I picked up Rose's mannequin and laid it gently on the worktable. Checking it carefully, I rotated the arms, since the keyhole shoulder fittings suffered the most risk of damage. After scrutinizing it,

I was relieved to find there were no major repairs needed. I tightened the fitting and worked the arm back into its socket.

I took the silk gown out of the bag and carefully tried it on the mannequin. I spent a good part of the morning to precisely pad the body; it took a practiced eye to look at the dress and know just how to shape the mannequin, but that's what made our figures so realistic. Burl made it easy with his fine nuances of the body's stance. He even captured that one of Rose's shoulders was lower than the other, and particularly the way she stood with her hip out. I slipped the dress on the figure to check the final fit. It looked like a perfect replica of Rose, minus twenty pounds.

Squinting at the figure, I knew something was wrong. What was it? I paused for a minute. Rose was not that wide-eyed in real life. "She needs eyelashes!" I laughed out loud and removed the head from the mannequin.

"Well, how was your Detective Adams?" Elise broke my concentration. I jumped and turned to face my mother, with Rose's head under my arm.

"How did you know I saw Dale?" I didn't give her time to respond. "But, yes, he came to the station. To make sure I gave my report I guess." I quickly changed the subject. "What do you think about this?" I held up Rose's head directly in front of her vinyl body.

Elise studied the soft, round features with the slightly crooked smile. "It's a very good likeness. It'll surely draw people to Rose's booth. Burl did a great job sculpting the head. You know how hard it is to capture an objective likeness when you know the subject; but he truly did another fine job." She nodded. "He got her grin just right."

"Yeah, he's come a long way with his sculpting. He was good when he first started, but remember they looked like store mannequins? Perfectly symmetrical. Now they look like people, don't you think? He's taken that step. I can feel Rose's soul when I look at this figure. And that's a talent not every sculptor has. I'm glad you found Burl."

"Actually, he found us," she reminded me.

It was true. Five years ago, during the time I was in Pennsylvania playing wife, socialite, and hostess to Dr. Reggie, I heard about the scene that Mario, our previous sculptor, had made when he quit in midsculpture on the largest job we had gotten to date. Elise was in a quandary, to put it mildly. Within a week of sending an SOS out through the artists' leagues and interviewing more than seven sculptors, Burl had just shown up on our doorstep, asking if we had any positions available. He knew of Montgomery Mannequins through the artists' grapevine, but hadn't heard of our immediate need. Ah, synchronicity! His years of decoy carving and portrait sculpting gave him experience that enriched his talent.

"Have you talked with him yet?" I looked at Elise and referred to the subject that caused us both the most grief. I still thought Burl would be a better owner of Montgomery Mannequins; he had a passion for making the figures look real. Maybe he would be swayed if Elise talked to him.

"That's not what I want, Laney. Or what Grandpa Albert would want. It was always Albert's intention that Montgomery Mannequins stay a family business. I wouldn't want to sell it to anyone, not even Burl."

"Well, I think it's a great idea." Maybe if I worked on them both, they would meet in the middle. I turned my back to Elise, and my attention to the Rose figure.

Chapter 12

*E*lise picked up her briefcase and moved toward the doorway of the clean room. "I'm off to my meetings now. Keep your fingers crossed on this one. This could be a big job." Elise's footsteps echoed toward the front door. I wished I could shrug off the topic as easily as my mother.

I turned my attention to Rose's eyelashes. It was always a challenge to place them just right, so the figure looked neither wide-eyed and startled, nor sleepy and sultry. This time, I got it right on the first try. I left the head propped on the worktable while I returned to the final steaming of the dress.

A banging on the front door made me jump and broke my concentration. I let in two uniformed policemen and led them to the sawdust evidence. Burl and I watched as they first laid down measuring tapes and took photos of every discernible footprint. Then they made notes that Burl's shoe size was a twelve and mine a seven. The whole thing lasted no more than fifteen minutes. They indicated that there was not much information to be gleaned from the sawdust, aside from what looked like a man's shoe, size ten. But no tread marks visible. At least I could report to Dale that I'd done my part.

It took the rest of the afternoon to finish the Rose figure, not counting the break I took for lunch at my desk and the three calls I returned to clients. Finally, I stood Rose on her feet and took a lint roller to the last bits of sawdust on her dress.

Elise popped her head in the door. I hadn't even heard her come back.

"How'd the meeting go?" I asked, surprised that she was alone. It was a better sign if the clients came to our studio for a tour or to finish up details of the contract.

"It looks promising. They showed me the blueprints of their museum and where they would like to put figures. Now they have to go for the funding."

"How many figures are they talking about?"

"I think fifteen. I need to give them a quote to include in their grant proposal."

She looked at the Rose figure. "Looks great, as usual. Another fine job, Laney."

"Thanks. Well, I'm off now. I have to stop in at Rose's shop to pick up her shoes and then I'll deliver this figure to her at the hotel. Don't hold dinner for me. I'll grab something with Rose."

"Doesn't Rose have her shoes with her?" Elise sounded preoccupied, and made it sound like Rose was at the hotel barefoot.

"Not *her* shoes. The matching shoes for this outfit." I chuckled, pulling a large plastic bag off the roll.

"Take a deep breath," I couldn't keep from saying to the Rose figure. Not only was it a long-standing joke since Grandpa Albert's time, but it had become my parting good luck wish for every figure we shipped off. I slid the plastic down the length of the figure, tying it at the bottom.

Elise chuckled. "You're just like your grandfather. He always talked to the figures as he built them too."

"I'll take that as a compliment." I smiled. "I've got to get to Rose's shop before Catherine locks up."

I grabbed the figure indelicately under the crotch with one hand and around the shoulders with the other, expertly flipping it across my center of gravity, and headed out the door. Down the hall, two women were leaving Rose's door, calling a parting goodbye to Catherine. They held the elevator door long enough to watch this four-legged creature come ambling toward them. I was accustomed to the looks I got when carrying the figures. I smiled and signaled to them not to hold the door, then propped the figure against the wall under Rose's Vintage Dresses sign. I leaned into the shop and called, "Catherine, I'm picking up Rose's shoes. See you later."

Catherine stepped out from her workshop in the back, into Rose's shop. "Oh hi, Laney! Do you have her figure? I'd love to see it."

"She's in the hallway. Come take a look." I retrieved the matching shoes from behind Rose's counter and met Catherine in the hallway. I smoothed out the plastic so she could have a good look.

"It's just great! It looks just like her. I know she's happy with it. Oh, and the iolite is perfect for the dress. It sets off the purple color well. I hadn't seen the pin on the dress yet. The last time I saw it was when I finished it and handed it to Rose. You know, I don't often get to see my finished jewelry on their dresses. Rose and I aren't always here at the same time."

The pin. On the dress. Again I wondered why had it been laying on my worktable last night? When I first left the studio and headed for my car, the pin was on the dress, hanging in the costume room. But when I went back inside to pick up the forgotten dress, that was when I was assaulted and was out for…how long was I out? I felt like it was only a few minutes. Then when I worked on the dress at home, the pin wasn't on it. The person who attacked me must have removed it from Rose's dress. And left it on the table. But who? And why?

Chapter 13

*O*ut in the parking lot, I put the back seat of my Civic hatchback down and carefully slid the mannequin in from the rear, once again glad I hadn't gotten rid of the old car. As small as it was, I could fit two figures in when I needed to. I just hoped the car would hold out for a few more years. The timing was bad for buying a new one, if I wanted to look at that old mansion near the Peabody Conservatory and The Walters Art Museum that was being converted into condos. I felt some guilt, helping reinforce the changing tenor of the city from low-rent studios to high-rent condos, but it was past time for me to be on my own again. I didn't like the thought of telling Carlos that I was one of those who helped him lose his studio, and Burl his apartment. I also didn't much like the thought of choosing between a new car and a new home.

As I neared the Redwood Hotel, I called the front desk and asked for Rose's room.

Rose answered, "'Lo?"

"Hi, Rose, I'm about two blocks away. Are you settled in for your big 'vacation'?" I laughed. I knew how much work these shows were. "And, the more important question, are you ready for dinner?"

"Yeah, to both. You wanna eat right now?"

"I'm starving. Let's just grab something quick before we set up the booth. I can't do it on an empty stomach. I'm going to park in the Pratt

Street garage. Meet me across the street in O'Shaughnessy's Pub in five minutes. We'll come back to the hotel and set up after we eat."

O'Shaughnessy's wasn't crowded at five o'clock. There were a few after-work drinks being enjoyed at the bar, but most of the stools were empty. The dark paneling and leather-look vinyl benches reminded me of a well-stocked library on a steamer. Lots of wooden trim around.

"I don't know why you like this place," Rose said. "It always smells like beer."

"And you, a local girl? Whatever happened to beer and crabs?" I chided her. I mean, who doesn't like steaming hot crabs with Old Bay seasoning and icy cold beer?

"Square peg, round hole. I'll take the crabs, you take the beer." Her crooked grin lit up her face.

The kitchen wasn't busy and the hot crab cakes came quickly. Rose told me, in between bites, about setting up her booth.

"I'm dying to see my mannequin. Let's get out of here," Rose said, swallowing the last mouthful. She slid her tip under her plate and herself out of the booth.

"I can't wait for you to see it. You'll love it, it's perfect. Even Elise says so." The light changed and we hurried across the street to the garage. The wind whipped around our faces.

"Still need Elise's approval?" Rose's eyebrows shot up.

"She's been in the business longer than I have." It sounded a lot like whining, and defensive whining at that. We both laughed.

"But you're an artist, Laney, trust your eye. Gran taught me that many years ago. By the way, how's the quilt business doin'?" Rose brought up my other love. Two of my friends had joined me in a fledgling business making quilts for beds as well as wall art. Mary-Taylor, with her background as a math teacher before her daughter was born, has an eye for patterns and details fitting together, and has a love of portraits and landscapes made from a myriad of shades of fabrics. Bea, with her jeweler's eye, chooses the fabrics with nuances of shades and hues, and she's a whiz with the sewing machine on the large pieces. I do the wall quilts, and since I drew the short straw, I also do the business end of things. We are officially called QuiltArts, which has become known in-house as the Quilt Tarts, or the Tarts for short. We have a small following, selling enough to barely afford studio space at the mill. It's just as well that we all still have our day jobs.

"It's slow going. We've got a few beauties finished right now, but we don't have any buyers. We're gearing up for an open house and sale. Bea has an interested party who might want to commission the Tarts.

"This new client, he's building a summer 'cottage' at Rehoboth Beach that's bigger than Elise's Victorian house in Carter's Village. We're trying to sell him on a quilt instead of a painting for his great room. It's going to take a good bit of our time, but it would help cover the rent and give us good exposure. We could use more jobs."

I slid the plastic-encased figure out of the back of the car and stood The Rose up, putting one hand on her shoulder to balance her.

"Okay, Rose, she's all yours." I bit my lip to keep from laughing.

Rose stepped up and put her hands around the waist of the figure.

"Oh no, Rose, she'll come apart at the waist if you pick her up like that. The proper way to carry your figure is one hand in the crotch and one hand around her back."

Rose stepped back. "Oh, right! I'm gonna grab this figure in the crotch!"

"Well, it's either that or she'll live in this garage forever."

"Well, shit!"

I dissolved into laughter, while Rose glared at me, and then slapped me on the shoulder.

I broke down and offered, "Okay, I'll help you. You take the feet and I'll take the shoulders. Just be careful she doesn't come apart at the waist and roll down the street!"

It was Rose's turn to laugh.

"It's true! It happened to me," I told her. "But only once. After that, I learned fast."

Two young men in suits walked by and tried not to stare. They stumbled over their conversation. I always got a chuckle out of heads turning when they saw someone carrying a body in a plastic bag down the street. *You gotta love your job.*

We lumbered down the sidewalk, looking like a couple of paramedics with a patient in evening garb and plastic wrap. Fortunately, the hotel had another door next to the revolving door, and a bellhop came to our rescue, holding it open. He didn't even blink at our cargo. We carried the figure inside and quickly spotted the elevator across the lobby.

"Don't look at the front desk," I whispered to Rose. It was always easier to just keep moving and avoid trying to explain. Rose set the mannequin's feet down at the elevator door.

When the doors opened, I scooped up the figure without waiting for Rose, stepped inside, and leaned it against the wall. Rose hurried in behind me. The elevator was the next big hurdle. A figure never failed to capture the attention of fellow passengers. I just looked at them and smiled, as if I lugged figures through public places every day. Which I did, nearly. I waited, expecting the classic comments, which came a moment later.

"Doesn't she get tired of holding her breath?" a man in the back said, seeing the plastic over the figure and laughing at what he thought was a joke I had never heard before.

I gave my pat answer. "No, she's used to it."

The elevator stopped on the next floor and emptied out. Figures often had that effect on crowds in an elevator. Rose turned to me and said, "Do you *ever* get used to people staring at you?" She said it in a whisper, even though we were alone.

"Never. But it doesn't bother me anymore. It's rather fun, in a perverse sort of way."

Rose led me to her booth in the meeting room housing the exhibit hall. I slipped the mannequin onto its stand and took off the plastic bag.

Rose looked at the figure with pride. "She's perfect, Laney."

Murder Among the Mannequins

A tall, blonde woman in the next booth wandered over. "Oh, what a great idea. This is going to steal the show. I'm glad I'm next to you—it will increase the traffic in our aisle."

"I hope so." This was the double-take factor Rose was counting on.

I backed up across the aisle and looked at the booth. I nodded, thinking, *Yes, this is a striking figure. It will surely attract attention.* I knew that later Rose would put the mannequin in the front of her dress shop, and it would become a draw for her there as well. When we first discussed the idea last summer, Rose had immediately loved it and had begun saving for her own mannequin. I convinced her that it was a business expense that would make her money in the long run. Besides, I'd explained, Elise thought it was great fun having her own double. I wish I felt the same about that figure of me that Elise was making now. I hadn't objected in the past when we used my face on figures to go into museums: my likeness has been a Civil War widow, a National Park ranger, and an 1890s bride, among other things. But at least I had held sway over past venues for my likeness—even turned down an offer for "me" to become a barmaid in Baltimore's red-light district. Perhaps I should have done that one; I could have invited Reggie and his doctor friends to the unveiling. Wouldn't that just crush his image! I laughed at the thought. On those few figures with my face that were already out there in the world, I had opted for different color hair or skin tone, so no one knew the face was mine but Elise, Burl, and me. It wasn't really me, more like a distant relative. But this new clone of me I wasn't ready for. I knew it was Elise's way of edging herself out and me in. I sighed.

84

Murder Among the Mannequins

Rose joined me across the aisle to survey her booth for finishing touches. Toward the front corner, a round table held a pink linen cloth draped to the floor, billowing out at the hem and tucked under the legs. A Lucite holder with her business cards announcing *Rose's Vintage Dresses, Fashion that Never Goes out of Style* sat in front of an impressive arrangement of burgundy chrysanthemums and white anthuriums. Three Victorian oak-and-cast-iron coat racks were strategically placed along the back wall of the booth, ready to hold the dresses she would display.

"Looks like you're ready. Before I go, I want to see the dresses you brought to display. That was the smartest thing for you to do—get a room here so you'll be fresh in the morning. I'll help you bring them down right now. Then all you have to do is show up here bright-eyed at 8:00 a.m."

"Thanks, Laney, I appreciate all your help. You know this is my first show. Come on upstairs. I brought a good selection of colors suitable for mothers of the bride. This year they're wearing the standard ivories and peaches, but also they're going toward the jewel tones. That's why I chose royal purple for my figure's dress."

Upstairs, Rose swiped her room key in the lock and leaned on the door handle. She flipped on the light switch and stopped in her tracks so suddenly that I bumped into her.

"Oh my God!" she shrieked. Over her shoulder I could see the dresses were in a heap on the floor. The empty dresser drawers were tossed on the bed. Her suitcases were lying open, their contents strewn around the room.

Chapter 14

"*D*amn! All my work!" she gasped, running over to the dresses. "Who would do this?" She picked up each one, briefly inspected it, and laid it across the bed.

I reached for a dress at my feet and looked at it. "Is anything torn or missing? Is the jewelry still on them?"

"If they're not, I'm in big trouble because most of them are stitched into the dresses. Look at this rhinestone buckle. See how it's stitched into the dress?" She held out a very wrinkled, taupe-colored crepe gown, turning it over to inspect it for damage.

Neither of us said a word for the next few minutes, unless you counted Rose's swearing. She picked up the last of the twelve dresses.

"I think you should call hotel security," I advised her, realizing we'd already disturbed the crime scene, if you could call it that.

"But nothing was taken! The gowns are all here, and the jewelry too. Mostly it will just cost me a few hours of steaming tonight. So much for a hot bath and an early evening!" Rose sat down hard on the bed, tears forming in her eyes.

"Doesn't matter. You may find a problem later, in which case you'll wish you had reported this. Also, it will alert them to keep a better eye on your room *and* your booth."

Rose sighed audibly as she picked up the phone.

"And ask them to put a guard in the vendor area tonight," I added. As Rose dialed the front desk, I wondered if I should call Dale. Even though he was in homicide, he would hear through the grapevine. It didn't hurt to have a friend in the force. I knew Rose would get extra attention if he put a word in.

Rose covered the mouthpiece with her hand. "I know what you're thinking, Laney. I can tell by the frown on your face. Don't bother telling Dale. This will be enough."

Into the phone, Rose continued, "Yes." She hesitated, and glanced at me. "And I want a different room!"

I gave her the thumbs-up sign.

"Not just a new key to this room. I'm packing up my things." She hung up the phone. "They're giving me a new room and sending security up to take a report. And they'll put an extra man in the show area tonight."

She flung herself back on the bed and punched the pillow.

I took the suitcase off the chair closest to the door and sat down to wait. It was less than five minutes before there was a knock on the door. Both of us jumped. Both of us laughed. I doubted the would-be burglar would return and politely knock.

"Yes?" Rose called, peering on tiptoes through the peephole in the door.

"Security, Miss Ebaugh." Rose peered through the peephole again and reached for the doorknob.

"You reported a break-in?" The man in the security uniform, whose badge said simply Security, was not much taller than Rose, and looked somewhere between eighteen and twenty-two. He was accompanied by a taller man in a suit and tie, whose name badge read D. Harbinger, VP Hotel Security.

"Yeah, someone was in here uninvited and made a mess of my room. But I don't think anything was damaged or stolen."

"Were you in the room at the time? Are you hurt?" The young security guard pulled out a notepad. He glanced up at Rose, genuine concern in his eyes. Rose, who was busily providing the details he requested, didn't seem to notice. "Alright. I'll have the hotel change your lock."

The older man, Harbinger, interrupted him. "No, we're giving you a new room as you requested. We want you to feel safe." As they left, he said to the younger man, "Bring Miss Ebaugh a key and escort her to her new room. I'll meet you in the security office." The door shut behind them.

Rose sighed but didn't make a move.

"Just sit. I'll do this." I was already gathering her gowns. By the time I got all her things packed up, the young security guard was back at the door with a new key. He led us up one flight, which made me feel better for some reason, her being on a different floor. I helped Rose unpack for the second time and offered to stay longer.

"No, I'm going to take that bath after all. And break open the minibar. I'll hang the gowns in the bathroom, and what the steam doesn't cure, I'll touch up by hand in the morning. Thanks, but all I need now is a good night's sleep. I'll talk to you tomorrow."

I pulled the door closed behind me until I heard a firm click, then headed for the elevator. I punched one, and on second thought, I poked my head out to look up and down the hall for any security cameras. As I stepped out into the lobby, I headed toward the front door. I spotted the security office just down the hall off the lobby and made a U-turn and, glancing at the front desk clerk whose head was buried in the computer screen, ducked down the hallway. Harbinger was just settling into his desk chair, looking unhappy, probably at the thought of the paperwork we caused him.

"Mr. Harbinger?" He looked up, startled.

"Is there a security camera on the floor where the break in occurred? Near the elevator perhaps?" I could only hope there was one pointed toward Rose's room but I hadn't seen one anywhere.

He let enough time go by that I thought he wasn't going to give me an answer, and told myself he didn't really owe me one. Still, I waited him out.

"And you need to know this why?"

"Because we'd like to know if this was a random hotel robbery—"

His voice grew louder. "Or what? Why would you think this was anything other than random? If you and Miss Ebaugh have some reason to suspect anyone, we need to know." He seemed anxious to be handed a reason to pin this on other than a thief targeting his hotel.

Again, I waited him out. I didn't want to mention what I was thinking . . . that this might somehow be connected to the break-in at my studio the other day. I wasn't convinced it was, but I wasn't convinced it wasn't either.

"No, I just thought you might have caught the person on tape," I hedged.

"Uh, our security tapes are just that, secure. For our use only, Miss…"

I could tell he wasn't going to let me see any tapes, digital or otherwise, if there were any. Instead of supplying him with my name, I threw a "thanks anyway" over my shoulder and left his office. I knew he must be concerned for the hotel's reputation, and this would get the hotel off the hook, so to speak, and not become news fodder.

During the drive home, my thoughts circled. Could there be a connection between the break-in at Montgomery Mannequins last night and the ransacking of Rose's room tonight? Nothing seemed to have been taken in either case. That was the weird part. What was so alluring at my studio *and* Rose's hotel room? It wasn't money. That's what was so puzzling. No money missing, no papers disheveled. The only common denominator was Rose's mannequin. But that didn't make sense. I knew I wouldn't figure this out tonight. I sighed and switched on the radio. Before I knew it, I was pulling into the driveway.

Murder Among the Mannequins

It was early the next morning when I arrived at Harbor Mill. There were no other cars in the lot, so I was surprised to see Ansel sweeping the first-floor hallway. He sometimes came in with Elise to do some odd jobs, but Elise wasn't in yet. I gave a quick wave and went upstairs. No one was in yet; there was no Burl humming in his workroom. I was eager to put the past two days' events behind me and get started on the next figure, Miss Prudence Suttler, Pioneer Woman.

I stopped in the office and dropped my bag in its usual spot next to my desk and my coat in its designated spot on my chair. I turned on my computer. This was going to be a great figure from what my research told me: As a child, Prudence Suttler had weathered the journey to the Wild West with her family in a covered wagon, and once there, she helped civilize those who were there before her and those who came after. What books they brought with them became a lending library for the town, and she became the first teacher. Her father had the foresight, and funds, to encourage the railroad to come to the West Coast by way of their town, and their fortune took off from there. Miss Pru gained a valuable combination of endurance, fortitude, and appreciation for the fine arts, and it was all reflected in her erect posture, deeply lined face, and blended gray-and-black hair pulled into a bun.

I needed to get the final details of the Suttler family down and e-mail the client. All this research always translated into a better figure. The more we knew about a subject, the closer we came with the sculpting and the costuming. Once I got this research out of the way, I could devote the rest of the day to what I liked doing best, working on the figure itself. Well, second best. I'd rather be working with the Quilt Tarts.

I called up my favorite search engine and typed in "Suttler." When I looked up, an hour had gone by, but I had gotten some great pictures and history on her.

"That's all the research I can stand for one day. Now on to Miss Pru herself," I announced to the empty office, standing up and hitting the print button before heading to the production room. The printer made its usual coughing, sputtering noises, but dutifully began printing. Yes! We got one more day out of the old thing.

I headed toward the door in the back corner of the office, the one that leads directly into the clean room without going through the storage area. I turned the doorknob and immediately banged my face on the door, which hadn't budged.

"Damn," I said to the empty office. "Who blocked this door?"

I backtracked through the office, checking the computer screen as I passed by. Two pages left to print. I picked up the top piece of mail from my desk, opening it absent-mindedly as I headed out of the office. I turned on lights in the storage area as I went. Immediately, the hands on the wall were lit up, causing me to think of the break-in the other night. Shaking off the thought, I walked past my design room, into the clean room. As I walked toward the large center worktable, my eye was drawn to the sun glinting off a piece of metal in the back corner of the room. There was a figure toppled onto the floor, and it was blocking the door from the office.

"Oh, so that's what the problem is!" I muttered to myself, walking over to right the figure. Suddenly my knees felt weak. A sword protruded from the figure's chest, a pool of blood surrounding it. I stifled a scream. This was no mannequin.

I stared down into the open eyes of Kalen Farrell.

Chapter 15

*W*arding off a nauseous feeling, I backed away from the body and groped for the nearest stable thing, the worktable.

I felt frozen in time. I had just met the man at Annie's two days ago, sitting with Catherine. What was he doing here? Kalen's left hand was across his chest, as if he had been clutching at the sword. His right hand was flung out to the side. I knelt beside him and put my fingers to his wrist, hoping I'd find a pulse. I noticed scratches on the outstretched palm of his hand. Suddenly I felt cold. I realized I'd examined many vinyl hands the same way, but I'd never gotten this chill down my spine.

"Oh my God." I took a deep breath and hurried back into the office. My knees gave way and I slid into my desk chair, knocking the mail onto the floor. *Calling the police twice in two days*, I thought as I robotically dialed 911. I didn't try to hide my sarcasm when I suggested to them that they might want to show up in a little quicker this time. I sat back in a daze. I felt like I was moving in slow motion. I didn't even hear the front door open.

"Laney, what's the matter?" I looked up to see Elise staring at me while she dropped her things on her desk.

I burst into tears just as the sirens screamed to a halt outside the mill. "At least the police are faster when there's a *body* involved."

"What?" Elise looked bewildered.

Several hefty police officers came puffing through the front door. They had made it up the stairs in record time. "What the hell?" Elise said, moving out of the way of the patrolmen.

"Are you the one who found the body?" The young one looked at Elise first, then at me. He looked like he hadn't been out of high school very long. God, everyone was looking like a kid these days. I was feeling old and suddenly tired. My knees were shaking. I grabbed the wastebasket and pulled it close; I still felt nauseous.

"Body?" Elise was even more bewildered this time. "What body?" she demanded to know.

The uniform ignored Elise and turned to me. "Where's the body? Are you the one who found it?"

I nodded numbly. I felt like I was moving slowly, like I was underwater. "I was working at the computer for an hour this morning," I stumbled over the words, "with the body lying in the room right next door to me." I pointed to the door in the back corner of the office and tried to keep my head from spinning and the nausea from welling up again.

"What body?" Elise nearly screamed.

A few more uniforms came in the front door, and I was relieved to see Dale right behind them. I vaguely gestured at the door in the back corner.

"Oh my God." Elise sat down. "Laney! Who is it? Not Burl!"

I shook my head.

"Do you know the victim, Laney?" Dale spoke in a kindly yet professional manner, walking toward the door at the back of the office. It was open just enough to see the body on the other side. He began writing in his tablet.

"His name is Kalen Farrell. I just met him this week. He's a friend of Rose's." I found myself standing and walking over to Dale, but at the same time feeling very tired and wanting to sit back down. By this time, Dale had pressed on the door with a gloved hand and opened it several inches, as much as he could without disturbing the body. I leaned against the wall. It suddenly smelled like death in the room. Even through the slightly open door, I could see the body. I hadn't realized how much blood was pooled on the floor around his chest. He was lying on his back with his head turned away from us, his eyes staring at the worktable, the sword protruding from his chest. I thought of his eyes across the lunch table two days ago and quickly looked away.

"Laney, I know you're upset. But I need you to tell me as much as you can."

I followed Dale back through the office, past the desk where Elise was sitting and fanning herself, and into the storage room. He stopped me at the door to the clean room. Elise had jumped up and was so close behind me, I could feel her breathing and hear her muttering, "Oh my God!" I felt her hand on my back, nudging me into the room.

"Laney, look around, is there anything missing or out of place?" It was Dale asking me, but I knew Elise was searching the room with her eyes for the answer.

I stood at the door and looked around the otherwise pristine room, glad for the distraction. I focused all my attention, and what little energy I had left, on the room itself—the shelves, the tools, the worktable. Anything but the body in the back corner with the jeweled sword handle sticking up several feet in the air.

Dale placed his arm around my shoulders, and I was glad to have him to lean on. He bent down to look directly into my eyes. "I know it's hard, but this is important. What can you tell me about the victim? Did he work here?"

I shook my head at the last question, while blurting out, "No, but he knows Rose and Catherine, down the hall."

"What about the sword, Laney?" he said softly. He seemed to be the old Dale I knew.

"It's ours. It's a prop. It goes with that Lafayette figure over there." I gestured to the other back corner, where a figure stood with an empty scabbard.

"Detective, there's somethin' here I think you oughta see," one of the officers standing over the body called to Dale. He was shaking his head.

I looked away as Dale walked over and spoke to the officer in a low voice. Dale squatted to look closely at the body. I busied myself with surveying the room. Look at anything but the body, I told myself. When did Kalen become "a body" to me?

Dale returned to me. "Laney, can you tell us anything else? Did you remove anything from the victim?"

I shook my head. "I noticed those scratches in his hand that you're looking at, but I certainly didn't touch anything."

Standing up and hiking up his belt, the young cop showed a marked resemblance to Barney Fife.

"Well, I don't see anything near the body. Miss Daniels, look around again. Is there anything that doesn't look right to you?" At least he was deferring to my knowledge of what looked right. He looked bored. He was too young to be jaded by this job.

I took a deep breath and looked around the worktable again. I was beginning to think more clearly, like I was waking up from a deep sleep. Nothing on the table; it was clean, just as I'd left it last night. The shelves still contained rows of "body hardware," the wooden arms and bins of screws and bolts. It all looked undisturbed.

My eye caught the open door in the back wall, the room where the costumes were kept. There was a heap of something lying on the floor in the normally organized room.

"Dale—uh, Detective Adams," I called. "I'd like to look at the room back there." I pointed to the costume room. "It looks like someone's been in there."

Dale walked me around the periphery of the workroom to the door of the costume room. I gasped at the disheveled mess; it looked like the end of a rummage sale. Dresses on the floor, hangers flung everywhere, boxes pulled off the shelves, their contents scattered. It looked like Rose's room last night, only worse.

"Damn it!" My voice sounded gravelly. Dale stopped me from picking up the dresses. Another officer was keeping Elise from coming in.

"We'll take photos first, Laney, and then we'll need you to go through and see if anything's missing." I felt the reality of it all, and the nausea, coming back.

"Sir, here's something," another officer called from the front door of the clean room. I couldn't tell one cop from another, there were so many of them. "Look at the dress on this dummy." He was standing in the front corner, next to Miss Prudence.

I followed Dale over to the Miss Prudence figure. The dress had been torn on the shoulder, and the costume brooch was missing. I hadn't even looked at this front corner of the room.

"Damn!" I said again. " There should be a pin on this dress. It looks like it's been torn off. It was one of Catherine's best."

"Is it valuable?"

"Depends on what you mean by valuable. It's just costume jewelry, but it's valuable to me. I can't send out this figure without it."

I finally let myself think about Kalen. I'd been holding him at arm's length in my mind up until now, refusing to think about this "body" as someone I knew. I winced as I rubbed my head.

"What's that knot on your head?" The young cop eyed me suspiciously. "Did you have a fight with the victim?" Suddenly I felt better, could think clearer. Leave it to a smartass to bring you to your senses.

"No!" *You twit*, I added in my head. "Someone broke into my studio last night and whacked me on the head in their attempt to get out." I couldn't help adding, "That time I called, but you guys didn't respond."

He ignored the jibe. "Did you see who it was?"

"No. There's a full report on it already on file. Ask your boss." I turned my back on the young officer.

"Are we through here?" I asked Dale.

"Yes, we're through with you for now, but it will take some time for the medical examiner and our guys to finish up here. And we need to take the sword with us."

"How long do you need to keep it? I have to ship the Lafayette figure soon."

"It will be a while. It's evidence."

"Keep it." I'd rather buy another sword than live with the thought of a murder weapon being part of a Montgomery mannequin in a museum.

Chapter 16

"Tom, why don't you and Thurgood start canvassing the other tenants in the building?" Dale said to the policemen. "See if anyone was here late. See if they saw or heard anything last night or this morning."

"Laney, I need to talk to this Catherine woman. The one who knows about this pin you mentioned."

"Catherine shares studio space with Rose Ebaugh, down the hall. Vintage Dresses. I'll show you where." I led Dale out to the main hallway. I felt better just walking down the hall, away from what had now definitely become a crime scene.

He paused at the grouping of realistic figures in the hall. "I'm always amazed by these things." I barely heard him. We stopped at the sign for Rose's Vintage Dresses. The door was open. I was surprised to see Howard inside. This was the second time I'd seen him here, looking rather moonfaced at Catherine. I made a small waving gesture.

"Catherine?" I called, stepping onto the carpeted floor. "You here?"

Catherine poked her head out from behind several racks of gowns.

"Hi, Laney, what're all the cop cars doing h…" Her voice trailed off as she spotted Dale and the two uniformed officers behind him. She spoke to Howard but didn't take her eyes off Dale.

"Excuse me, Howard. I guess I need to speak to Laney."

Howard hesitated before leaving the shop. My brain snapped into focus, in that Catherine didn't yet know about Kalen. I walked to the back, through the racks of dresses, and came to the door of Catherine's workroom. Dale followed close behind. "This is Detective Dale Adams. Can we go into your workroom?" I said, not knowing how to begin.

"Of course," she said, waving us in.

"This is Detective Adams," I repeated. "He has some questions for you."

"For me?" Catherine's face reflected her bewilderment, but she ushered us into her workroom. I had been in Rose's dress shop plenty of times, but had only gone to the back, into Catherine's jewelry workshop, once or twice. The previous tenant had put up a wall across his space, dividing the single shop into two with a door in the middle of what was now Catherine's front wall. The back room was a small studio, about fifteen feet by twenty feet. It was made smaller by a tiny bathroom built into one front corner, and in the other front corner, a desk filled with papers and books on jewelry and travel. Across most of the back wall, along the bank of windows, was a workbench with trays of jewelry findings, tools, and gemstones. Except for the crooked stacks of books on her desk, the workspace was organized and tidy.

"Catherine, sit down," I began. She lowered slowly onto the loveseat-sized couch in her workroom. Her eyes moved from my face to Dale's.

Dale went into full detective mode. "Miss Gilbert-Smith, I need to ask you some questions. What time did you get here today?"

Catherine furrowed her brow and looked back at me.

I gave Dale a look to let him know I didn't give a damn about protocol; I was going to be the one to tell Catherine. There was no easy way to say it, whatever her relationship was to Kalen, so I sat down next to her and reached for her arm.

"Kalen's dead!" I blurted out.

"What?" She sat stunned, looking from me to Dale. Clearly she didn't comprehend what I said, or maybe she just didn't believe it.

Dale glared at me and pulled me back toward the door. "I'll take it from here, Laney. And I'll talk to you later." He was clearly dismissing me.

I didn't know what he was worried about. It's not like I mentioned her missing pin. But it was clear that I was no longer needed.

"Call me later," I called as I headed for the front of the dress shop, pulling her studio door closed behind me. As I walked past Rose's étagère display case just inside her front door, I stopped dead in my tracks. I couldn't believe my eyes. There was Miss Prudence's topaz brooch! The one that was torn off her dress in my studio!

I opened the glass cabinet door and reached in for the pin. What was it doing here? My head was spinning. Just last night it was on Miss

Prudence's dress in my clean room. How did it get here? And why? When? And by whom? Why would Catherine or Rose have taken it back? And how did they get it? Oh God, one of them wouldn't have killed Kalen, would they? I thought back to the argument in the parking lot.

"Well, you've had some excitement here this morning." I jumped as a voice very close to my ear interrupted my thoughts. "What's going on?"

Instinctively I took my hand out of the cabinet. The glass door made a snapping sound when it closed. I looked up into Bea's face. I hadn't realized I was holding my breath until I exhaled. Bea! I was glad to see my fellow Quilt Tart. She was the perfect person to ask about the pin.

"Bea, I'm so glad you're here; I need your jeweler's eye. Look at this pin and tell me what you think," I whispered.

She pushed a stray hair behind her ear. "Wow. Nice topaz!" She whistled, peering in to have a closer look.

"Shhh!" I was afraid Dale would hear us, and I wanted to get Bea's opinion first.

"This was taken from a murder scene. It's a piece of costume jewelry that Catherine made for me. The last time I saw it, it was in my studio, and that was just last night. It was on a dress in my workroom. What the hell is it doing here?"

"Wait . . . back up . . . are you telling me that there was someone murdered? In your studio?"

I nodded.

"Last night?"

I nodded.

"Who?"

"I came in this morning and found Kalen Farrell's body in the clean room."

"Kalen Farrell? Isn't he that friend of Catherine's?"

Again I nodded.

"Well, that explains the parking lot full of cops! Let me see that pin." Before I could stop her, Bea reached in and picked up the pin by its edges with two fingers, brought it out, and gently balanced it in her left palm. She pulled out a loupe from one of the many overstuffed pockets in her smock. She brought the pin to within an inch of her nose, with the loupe between it and her eye. It sounded like she didn't know Kalen well, but even so, I was surprised that her interest in the stone overshadowed any interest in a dead body.

She whistled softly. "Those small stones are glass, but that large one is a gen-u-ine topaz." She pulled the word into three distinct syllables.

"What? You mean it's real?"

"It's real all right. Relatively valuable, too, I'd say, judging from the size and the slight reddish-gold color. Maybe five hundred dollars. And that's wholesale."

"For just the center stone?" I was astounded.

"Yep!"

Just then the door behind us opened and Dale and Catherine emerged into Rose's shop.

I quickly took the pin from Bea's hand by its edges. Keeping my back to Dale, I returned it to the shelf and quietly shut the glass door. Turning around to face them, I noticed Catherine looked remarkably calm.

Dale headed out of the shop. "Laney." He nodded to me. "I'll be in touch."

"You know where to find me." I moved aside to let him pass, but still blocked his view of the brooch. I wasn't sure why I was being so protective of it.

Chapter 17

I looked at Catherine, my back still to the display case. The silence spoke for itself.

"I can't believe Kalen's dead." Catherine stated it matter-of-factly, and her shoulders visibly relaxed. "I'm only sorry that you were the one who found him, Laney. That must have been awful."

"I've had better mornings. You heard that Miss Prudence's pin is missing?"

"That's what Detective Adams said. He asked me about its value."

"And what did you tell him?"

"That it's just costume jewelry, like all my pieces. You know I get my stones from flea markets and thrift stores. I don't have anything more expensive than the Italian glass beads I use—maybe twenty dollars apiece." Catherine turned and walked back toward her workshop, her words trailing off. Bea and I stared at her back and then glanced at each other. Her nonchalance was piquing, to say the least.

"How did it get here?"

"What are you talking about?" Catherine turned. She sounded more annoyed than puzzled.

"Take a look for yourself." I stepped aside and opened the glass display case.

Catherine picked up the pin, her mouth open, but no words came out.

"How did it get here?" Catherine asked me just as I asked her the same question. Again. We looked up at each other.

Catherine was the first to speak. "Didn't Rose give it to you? I finished it and gave it to her early this week. I knew you had a deadline, and I didn't want to be the one to hold you up." She paused and then said, "Maybe Rose put it here until she could get it to you?"

"No, Rose gave it to me on Monday, the same time she gave me Miss Pru's dress. The weird thing is, it was on the Miss Prudence dress in my studio yesterday. When I came in this morning, it was gone. Torn right off the dress. And Kalen . . . Kalen was dead on the floor." I paused, hoping for an explanation. When none was forthcoming, I prompted Catherine, "How did it get back here?" *And why?* I wondered.

"I haven't seen it since I gave it to Rose." Catherine sounded defensive, but also perplexed. .

Bea spoke up gently. "We know it's a real topaz, Catherine. What are you doing using a real stone like this in with glass in a piece of costume jewelry?"

A look passed between them, and suddenly I felt like the outsider.

"You might want to have a seat," said Catherine. "This is a long story."

We retreated to the couch in her workroom. She started to pace. I'd never seen Catherine anything but totally in control before.

"I started out making my costume jewelry from beads and stones I got at estate sales and flea markets. I'd dismantle them from their old settings and create new designs, mostly pins, pendants, and earrings. Kalen started bringing me what he claimed were beads he found at street markets and secondhand markets in Italy. I didn't have any reason to suspect anything was wrong. I was grateful. It cut down on the time I had to devote to searching out old jewelry, and gave me more time at the bench.

"So he's my main source, or to be more accurate, I guess I became his fence—to set the stones he comes—came—up with."

You could have heard a pin drop as Bea and I stared open-mouthed at her. I was trying to absorb this news. I really didn't know Catherine at all!

"A while back, I started suspecting some of Kalen's sources. You know, my degree in finance didn't include classes in gems," she said wryly. "I just know what I've learned from my flea market finds and my trips to Italy."

"At first, he just gave me a couple of loose stones. Then he gave me a few old brooches to dismantle and set into new pieces, mostly earrings and pendants. They started coming fairly regularly. He began giving me some of the most gorgeous pins and rings, and he sometimes seemed to know what he was going to be able to get beforehand. As if he had a ready source, instead of finding them secondhand, as he claimed. When I asked him how he knew what he was going to get ahead of time, he told me he was helping out some of his financial clients at Gilbert

Strickland, older ladies who needed to supplement their income. He offered to buy their jewelry for cash."

She shook her head. "All this while working at my father's firm. He said the old ladies wouldn't dare sell it through a jewelry store. They all shopped at Kirkland Fine Jewelry, and even though Kirkland has a generous trade-in policy, they needed cash. He paid them a "pittance," he bragged, *and* they filed insurance claims. Against insurance policies he had sold to them, he was happy to tell me."

"So why did they do it?" Bea wanted to know.

"If they went to Kirkland, they wouldn't get cash for the pieces, and they were afraid word of their financial situations would leak out to their circle of friends. That was paramount to them—keeping it quiet. I realized that was why he wanted the pieces reset, so they couldn't be traced. But I thought it was legitimate, you know? I didn't know about the insurance fraud. Just thought he was doing it on the QT, and I could understand that.

"But Kalen started getting more and more demanding—tighter time frames, always asking if I had told anybody, so finally I confronted him."

Catherine choked up and hesitated. Then she plowed ahead. Actually she went back to the beginning.

"It started when I was in college. I spent a semester in Italy, and Kalen was renting a villa in the same town. We were close for the summer, but then we had a falling out. I never saw him after I left Italy; I didn't even know he lived in Baltimore, until I finished college and went to work for my father at Gilbert Strickland. I was quite shocked, not to mention irritated, when Kalen got hired. I hadn't known anything about him really when we were in Italy, and certainly not that he was married. He had told me he was from Chicago, was divorced, and was taking a break between jobs. Why would I not believe him?"

Catherine stared off over my head, as if reliving that time.

"At first it was easy to avoid him at work. But then he started with the requests for setting stones. He just kept after me. So I didn't press it; I just set the old ladies' jewels for him. I didn't want to know any details; figured what I didn't know wouldn't hurt me. I would just reset whatever he gave me and give the pieces back to him and keep my nose out of it."

Bea spoke up. "Was he stealing the gems from Kirkland?"

I knew Kirkland Fine Jewelry was a large venerable Baltimore company, but otherwise I wasn't following Bea.

"Why would you think he stole from Kirkland?"

Bea clued me in. "He's married to Alison Kirkland. Don't you read the society section of the newspaper?"

Catherine shook her head slowly. "I don't know. Maybe he was stealing from them; maybe he was reselling the newly set pieces through them. I just don't know."

I heard a sort of whistle escape my lips. "Oh boy, I knew Kalen was smooth when I met him at lunch. I just didn't know how smooth. What a creep!" I said it mostly to myself, afraid of what was coming next. "So what the heck were you doing going to lunch with him last week? I thought you must be friends."

Catherine put her head in her hands and continued. "More like 'business colleagues' or 'partners in crime' I guess. It took me a while to face it, but finally, just last week, I told him not to bring me any more of his stones. I was feeling more and more uncomfortable and pressured. I had to face the probability that the jewelry was hot, and I wanted out." She took a deep breath and sat there a minute, staring at the wall behind me. Her face softened with resignation and her lip began to quiver. I still didn't understand why she went along with it, why she didn't report her suspicions to the police.

She must have read my thoughts. "He's been blackmailing me into resetting his pieces."

Bea and I continued to stare at her open-mouthed. *Oh shit!* I thought, *This just keeps getting worse and worse,* but it came out as "What?"

I had no idea she'd been in this kind of trouble because of Kalen. My guess was Bea and even Rose didn't either.

Catherine continued, "I had finally had enough of Kalen's manipulation. I didn't want to be part of this, no matter what it cost me. He told me that I didn't have a choice; that I would reset anything he brought to me and keep my mouth shut." A tear rolled down her cheek.

I knew Catherine had worked at her father's company after college and had soon given that up for her first love: working with gems and stones and beads. That's how Rose found her—to use her jeweled pins and buckles in her dresses. And that's why I thought of her to set the stones in Lafayette's sword handle. The sword that became the murder weapon.

112

The sword that was being looked at by the police. Right now. Her prints would be all over it. Mine too, and possibly Elise's and Burl's.

"That's when Kalen admitted the gems were stolen, that I had been a—what did he say—an 'accessory to stolen goods.' Laney, I had been part of his operation for a year and didn't even know it. But who would believe that? I feel like such an idiot." She was sobbing audibly now.

I shifted uncomfortably. My heart went out to her, but was I being manipulated as well?

Chapter 18

"*K*alen gave me a beautiful smoky-red, amber-colored stone several weeks ago and told me to keep it until he decided what to do with it. And he had warned me against showing it to anyone. He was being so secretive about it. That should have been a clue right there. But I guess I just didn't want to see it."

Catherine choked back a sob, but continued. "Then when Rose asked me to duplicate the pin in the Prudence photo, I decided that I would use that stone Kalen was so protective of—it would be perfect for it—and to hell with him. I wanted it out of my studio. I knew the figure would be long gone by the time he found out. And what was he going to do, turn me in? Report it stolen? Ha!"

She continued, "But Laney, when you let it out of the bag at lunch that Rose had used the topaz gem in a pin, he was furious! I took great pleasure in telling him that it was already on one of Rose's dresses and he would never see it again. Needless to say, he didn't take the news too well." Catherine held up her wrist to display a hand-sized bruise.

I sat back against the soft pillows. I thought about the argument I'd witnessed in the parking lot at Annie's. So this was what it was about. Perfect hindsight made me wish I'd stepped in, though I don't know what good it would have done.

"Did you tell this to Dale—er, Detective Adams?" I knew the answer already.

"Not yet."

I was biting my lip so hard I could taste blood. I truly didn't know what to do. On the one hand, I felt some allegiance to Dale. On the other, I wanted to believe that it was Kalen's doing, that he got what he deserved, that Catherine wasn't capable of stealing or lying. Or murder. I knew this looked bad for her. What I decided to do was nothing. For now. I convinced myself I wasn't really withholding evidence; I was thinking things through.

Catherine's shoulders sagged even more. "I guess I need to talk to Detective Adams. Get him to see I'm not hiding anything."

I realized that Rose was at the trade show and still didn't know about Kalen's death, and I didn't want her to find out about it the way Catherine did. But I also didn't want to interrupt her trade show day. First, I'd try to catch Burl to see if he knew anything. I walked back down the hallway, past the figures display, heading to my office, but was stopped by yellow crime scene tape across the doors. It was a stark contrast to the elegant gold script spelling out Montgomery Mannequins.

So with no other choice, I found I was relieved to have some downtime until I could find Elise or Burl. On the first floor, I pushed open the heavy doors and, dodging the rain that had started, headed toward home. What had Kalen been doing in my studio? Was he after the topaz brooch? If so, why did it end up in Rose's shop? How did it get there? Did Kalen put it there before he died? It all made no sense.

Just as I pulled into my driveway, I saw Ted carrying a bag of soil toward the back corner of the house. Good, he was taking care of the roses. We'd be ready for next year's garden tour. "Hi, Ted," I called a greeting. "Is Elise in the house?" I didn't see her car, but sometimes she parked over under the trees.

"Yes, she came home a little while ago." He hesitated, as if unsure of saying what was on his mind. "I heard about the body you found." He sounded apologetic, concerned.

"It was awful! At first I thought it was one of the mannequins that had fallen over. But then I saw the blood." I shuddered, reliving the scene.

"Who could have done it? And why? And why in your shop? Do they have any theories?" He asked all the questions I didn't have answers for, and we were both getting wet.

I shook my head. "None that they're sharing with me. Or with Mom. I'll talk to you later, Ted," I said as I edged in the front door. "I'll let you know when I find out more."

Inside, I could hear Elise banging pots and pans in the kitchen. I found her surrounded by every cooking utensil she owned spread out on the counters, with the cabinets empty. Cleaning and organizing was her go-to task when she had big things on her mind. She claimed it helped her think.

She started right in talking to me, even though she hadn't yet turned around.

"Who would have killed that man? And why?"

That's when she turned abruptly and said to me, "Why in the world was he in our studio?" When I shrugged and opened my mouth to answer, she continued, "Isn't he the man you just met at lunch the other day? The one who was with Catherine?"

I nodded. "Umm-hmm." I waited for her to finish venting.

"What in the hell was he doing in our place? How did he get in? The lock wasn't forced, the police said. Does he know Burl?"

"I don't think so." But I wondered the same thing myself, and headed for my quarters. The thing I needed most right now was peace and quiet, and I wasn't going to get it in the kitchen. Jesse followed me into my room. After five minutes of attempted quiet, during which I paced around the room, sat down, stood up, paced some more, and sat down again, with Jesse following along right behind me, I got up, returned to the kitchen and plopped down at the table. I watched Elise arrange and rearrange the china in one of the cabinets.

She started in as though I hadn't left the room. "It's just so annoying and unsettling. Why would he break in to our studio? What could we possibly have of value to anyone? Our computer is a dinosaur, we don't keep cash around, and I cannot imagine a figure being of that much interest to anyone but the client who commissioned it." She was slowing down with the pot crashing as she neared the end of the kitchen rearranging.

I felt it was time to tell her what I knew.

"Sit down, Mom." I got up to put some coffee on. "I'll tell you what I know. After I had lunch with Rose at Annie's the other day, I overheard Catherine talking to Kalen in the parking lot. Actually, it was more like Kalen raising his voice to Catherine. I saw him holding her by the wrist, and when he spotted me looking at them, he abruptly let go. She's got a bruise to prove it."

"I thought they were friends."

"Me too, but apparently not. Or as they say, 'It's complicated.'" I poured two cups of coffee and joined Elise at the kitchen table. That's when I got my quiet time. We sat there pondering the whole situation, not saying a word. After awhile, I got up and put my coffee cup in the sink.

"I don't understand any of it!" Elise shook her head.

"I need to clear my head. I'm going out. I think I'll walk down to the village."

"Why don't you take a look at the old pharmacy on Chandler Street? I've got to meet the architects there in an hour. You can see what we're planning. In fact, I'd like your opinion."

Again with the restaurant! What I'd really have liked to do was to walk in the other direction, but I guessed it was time to stop dragging my feet. I knew it was futile trying to talk her out of it. I was trying to be happy for Elise going after her retirement dream. I really was happy for her restaurant, but the retirement part—not so much.

It had stopped raining, so I put on my running shoes and grabbed Jesse's leash. Jesse was at the front door before I could put my slicker on, vacillating between sitting patiently at the front door and whining to nudge me along. Hartmann Avenue was slick and had no sidewalks, so we walked in the street. There was no traffic at this time of midday, actually very little car traffic anytime of day. Once we finally got to Chandler Street, after multiple stops dictated by Jesse, we turned left. Chandler Street, often referred to here in the business district as Main Street, was busy with people heading to shops and shopkeepers welcoming them in. The pharmacy was at the far end of the street of old storefronts, just past the library and the municipal parking lot. I knew that was one of the draws for Elise, the parking right next door. The front of the building had a recessed center door, inset between two windows that jutted out to the sidewalk. These windows had once housed medical supply displays, but now Elise was talking about redoing the floors so that she could put a small table and two chairs in each window. Jesse and I passed it by and headed for the park, another two blocks. I'd been reneging on my promise to give her more exercise, and this was as good as anytime to get back to it. We jogged around the perimeter of the park for twenty minutes until one of the benches surrounding the playground beckoned. Twenty minutes was a good start on my new promise to Jesse, I figured.

I couldn't believe it was only yesterday afternoon that I had taken Rose's figure to her at the Redwood Hotel. Her room being tossed and then a murder in my studio! I was having trouble wrapping my brain around all this, especially the murder. What was Kalen doing in Montgomery Mannequins? I felt offended by my space being violated. He had a lot of nerve being killed in my studio! Why had he broken in? And how did he get in with no forced entry? And who killed him?

My thoughts were going in circles, with no answers.

I couldn't get the image of Kalen's body out of my head—the pool of blood, the sword protruding from his chest. The sword that Dale took for analysis. It would have my fingerprints all over it! Elise's too. Catherine's also, and maybe Burl's and Rose's! Great! That made us all suspects.

My head was spinning. I needed answers.

Chapter 19

I cut Jesse's walk short and headed back to the pharmacy building—I was having trouble thinking of it as a restaurant. I promised Elise some opinions this morning. Elise was inside, deep in conversation with two architects. I heard someone moving furniture around in the back corner. It was Ansel, sweeping the floor and moving some stray chairs around. He seemed to show up when I least expected to see him. Jesse headed straight back to him.

We talked for two hours, or rather Elise and the architects talked. I listened, only interjecting a few comments when Elise called for them. I have to admit, I was beginning to feel some of Elise's enthusiasm. Jesse was tugging me toward the door, so I knew she was at the end of her patience.

I waved to let Elise know I was leaving and Jesse and I hit the pavement. It was about time to tell Rose about Kalen. The rain droplets were starting again, so Jesse made fewer stops, and the walk home was quicker than the walk there. I toweled off Jesse, filled her water bowl, and left her comfortably gnawing on a rawhide bone.

It was a little before four when I left for the Redwood Hotel. This time I parked in the hotel's underground parking lot and took the elevator to the lobby.

When I got to Rose's booth, she was just finishing up with an interested mother-of-the-bride-looking woman.

"Hi, Laney. I didn't expect you today." Rose looked pleasantly surprised. She looked remarkably current in a silk faille shirtwaist dress circa 1940. Those forties styles gave her a waistline.

"Thought I'd see if you needed a break. What time can you leave here?"

"Officially, we stop at five. But as you can see, attendance is already tapering off."

"Let me take this last forty-five minutes for you. Go take a shower and rest. Then I'll treat you to dinner." The time went by quickly, even though there were only two semi-interested people who took Rose's business card and moved on. I busied myself with taking note of the other types of booths there. There were the expected services at a wedding trade show: caterers, limousines, florists, and photographers, but I couldn't help wondering if the insurance man and home repair man had had any interest.

Promptly at 5:00 p.m., Rose showed up, dressed in her comfortable fallback denim jumper and looking much better than I felt. We tossed protective plastic over the dresses in the booth and headed out the door. In the lobby, Rose suggested eating in the hotel restaurant. That suited me fine, since I wasn't particularly hungry and it was convenient. The hostess took us through the crowded bar and seated us at a table in the dining room, away from the only other occupied table in the place.

"Ah, the end of a long day!" Rose sighed and stretched her arms.

"I didn't know how hard it is to be on your feet all day."

I smiled weakly.

"Laney, what's the matter? You look pale. Are you okay?"

I didn't know how to begin, so I didn't. "Tell me about your day, Rose. I'd like to hear how the show went." I was feeling partly responsible for Rose's success or failure since I was the one who encouraged her to spend the time and money to do this show. The waiter brought a Diet Coke for Rose and a Coors Light for me. I took a long gulp and enjoyed the smoothness going down my throat.

"It went great. I think. It was pretty busy all day. And you were right about 'The Rose' mannequin. I spent much of the time telling people about having it made, about how Burl sculpted my likeness and made and poured a mold. But they always ended up looking at my dresses! I made lots of appointments for people to come into the shop to be fitted, including Mrs. Edmund Munroe's daughter."

"The Mrs. Munroe of the society pages?" Wow, that was something!

"Yep. She booked time for her daughter and seven bridesmaids! Seven! She wants the whole wedding to be a 1940s theme," Rose bubbled over. "Laney, thanks for suggesting I get the mannequin. This job alone will pay for it!"

The waiter returned and we gave him our orders. After he left, I decided the time to tell Rose was now or never.

"I'm glad you had such a great day, but I've got some bad news." I reached over and put my hand on Rose's arm.

"What!?" It was more a command for me to spill it than a question.

My throat cracked, and I took a sip of water to clear it. "Kalen's dead," I said simply.

"What?" she said, trying to comprehend. "Kalen? Dead?"

"And I was the one who found him. In the clean room."

"The clean room!" she echoed. "*Your* clean room?"

I nodded.

"Oh my God. How did it happen? When?"

"That's the terrible part. I found him this morning. He was stabbed with the sword from one of our figures."

"How is Catherine taking it?"

I thought that was an odd comment since I hadn't gotten to the part about the missing pin or talking to Catherine. "She seems a little shaken. Why?"

"Laney, sometimes you are so dense. Haven't you noticed he stops in a lot? In our shop?"

"No. I've never seen him before the other day at Annie's."

There was silence from both of us.

"What are you telling me?" I paused, and then it just tumbled out. "I know about the gems."

"What about the gems?" Now it was Rose's turn to look blank.

"Apparently the stones Catherine gets from Kalen are real." I told her about Bea looking at the pin.

"You're kiddin', right?"

When I shook my head, she whistled under her breath. "Well that answers lotsa questions. That man had more facets than a diamond!" Rose laughed at her own joke. "I knew they'd had an affair, but there didn't seem to be a lot of love in it. A strange relationship if you ask me."

Now it was my turn to look dumbfounded. We both sat there, absorbing it and sorting it all out. So Catherine had had an affair with Kalen, probably in Italy, and now she was being used by him to help fence stolen gems. The fact that they had an affair was no big deal, at least not for Catherine, I figured. But what about Kalen's wife? Would Alison kill her husband to protect the Kirkland name? Or Kirkland Fine Jewelry's standing in the community? Could Catherine have threatened Kalen, or killed him? I took another swallow of beer.

I filled Rose in on Miss Prudence's torn dress and the missing pin and then finding the pin in her display case, which she seemed to be genuinely unaware of. Then I got to my other point.

"I wanted to be the one to tell you about Kalen. You'll be getting a visit from the police since the pin was found in your shop. That is, once I tell them it's there."

"You didn't tell them? Not even Dale?" Rose's eyebrows shot up. "No."

Rose stared at me. I suddenly realized how that sounded.

She slammed her hand down on the table. "You think I'm guilty!" She stared right through me and heaved a great sigh. "I have to go." Rose abruptly stood up to leave, her dinner only half-finished. Her eyes narrowed in disappointment. "I can't believe you think I had anything to do with this!"

"No! Wait, Rose, it wasn't like it sounds! I'm going to tell Dale. I know you're not guilty and I sure didn't want Dale to think you were. I was just trying to sort things out first." I left the rest of my dinner too, tossed two twenties on the table, and hurried into the lobby behind her. I caught her arm as she was entering the elevator and gently pulled her back.

"Hold up, Rose. You know I'm on your side."

"What the hell are you talkin' about? My side? I don't have a side! You're just now tellin' me someone was murdered in the mill, and just because the damn pin was found in my shop, you think I did it?" She yanked her arm out of my grasp, heaved a deep breath, and looked away. The lobby was busier with people now, so I led her to a secluded corner. She took another deep breath.

"Of course I don't think you did it! I'll talk to Dale first thing tomorrow morning. Get some sleep." I hugged her, and left her to go up to her room.

Chapter 20

I awakened early the next morning after a night of tossing and turning. I dressed and took Jesse for a run around the property. We hit the dirt driveway, heading back toward the woods past the old barn. Running helped me clear my head, and being in the woods helped me relax. I realized exercising Jesse was as much for me as for her. I didn't look forward to telling Dale I had seen the pin yesterday, let alone handled it, but I knew I had to right this. Now. We got to the far end of the old driveway where it emerged through the trees onto Hartmann Avenue. We turned left because, although it was uphill, it was shorter than winding back through the woods. Jesse and I broke into a jog until we reached the paved driveway. Then we slowed to a cooldown walk down the drive and around to the back door.

I fed and watered Jesse in the kitchen and hoped it wasn't too early to call Dale.

"Hello?" he said in a gravelly voice.

"Can you meet me at Annie's for breakfast? I need to talk to you."

"Sure. When?"

"An hour?"

"Okay." It sounded like he dropped the phone, and I hoped he hadn't just slammed it down.

I showered and dressed quickly and headed downtown.

"I know, I know. I should have told you sooner," I said to Dale for the fifth time as I pushed my breakfast around on my plate. I had finally stopped trying to explain and just let Dale vent. A couple of minutes later, when I could get a word in, I apologized. Again.

Dale finally spoke in a calm voice. "Let's look at all that's happened in the last week. First, someone broke into Montgomery Mannequins that evening you started to go home but then went back in for something you forgot, right?"

"But that wasn't related. Was it?"

"Never discount anything, Laney. It's all a possibility until it isn't." He paused.

"Okay, so someone obviously waited until after you left to enter the premises, and when you returned unexpectedly, he—let's assume it's a he, someone big enough to overpower you—knocked you down and fled before you could see who it was."

"Right."

"Second, the next day, Rose's hotel was tossed."

"I thought that was just a random break-in. Nothing was taken; she hadn't left any valuables in her room. But now I wonder if they're related. Someone was looking for something, the way they left both places ransacked."

"That's right. You've heard me say there are no coincidences.

"Third, Kalen was murdered on the premises of Montgomery Mannequins. That was the same night, right? You found him the next morning?"

"Right." I didn't like that it was becoming easy to talk about murder.

"And now you're telling me that an item—this pin—that had been in your studio the night before is now *not* in your studio?"

"Right."

"*And* you touched it? The pin? Damn it, Laney. You could be charged with obstruction!"

There was a lull while Dale finished off his eggs. My brain was still whirling. He gulped down his coffee.

"Well, the door wasn't forced, so is it still breaking and entering? And how did he get in? We had locked up for the night." *And why?* I couldn't help thinking. I rubbed my forehead.

"I'm the one that's supposed to be asking the questions, Laney. In fact, I shouldn't be discussing it with you at all."

I just sat there looking at him, waiting for him to be the first to break the uncomfortable silence, a trick he had taught me. I didn't think it would work on him, but he finally continued in a hushed voice.

"Look, all we know right now is he got inside somehow without breaking the door in. We know he was killed. We know where and how, but we don't know why or by whom." He paused, and then continued, "And now we know about the pin that was torn off the dress and moved, but we don't know if that has anything to do with anything. That's how it stands.

"I'll send Thurgood right over to get the pin. Don't touch it again!" he warned, sharply. "I have another appointment right now. Gotta run. Thanks for breakfast." He got up and reached for his jacket, swinging his leg over the back of his chair in a John Wayne sort of move. I was amazed at his agility. He turned and was out the door, leaving silence in his wake.

I was left to ponder things. Why exactly had I hidden the pin from Dale? I didn't know the answer to that myself. I didn't really think Rose had anything to do with Kalen's murder. I didn't know Catherine that well, but I tended to think the same of her.

But why had Kalen been in my studio two nights ago? How did he get in? He must have realized his topaz was about to be sent off to a new home, never to be seen again. It's the only thing that would tie everything together: Rose's hotel room being ransacked and her gowns dumped on the floor; the disheveled mess in the costume room in Montgomery Mannequins when Kalen was killed; and, come to think of it, even before the ransacking at the hotel, when someone was in my studio knocking me out when I went back in to pick up Rose's dress, the fact that the only thing amiss was a few mannequins and their costumes.

Kalen *must* have been after the topaz brooch; it was torn off of Miss Pru's dress and he had scratches on his palm. But how did the pin get from Miss Prudence's dress in my studio to the étagère in Rose's shop? None of this seemed to worry the police very much, but it was really

bothering me. In fact, the more I thought about it, the tighter my grip on it became. I felt used, and I didn't like it. It was *my* studio that now held blood on the old floorboards. Would it leave a stain forever? It was *my* company that would now be known as that place where someone was killed. It was *my* friends who were under suspicion.

Which led me to think about Catherine—why didn't she get away from Kalen in the last year if she felt manipulated by him? She seemed to be a bright, independent person; a little self-centered perhaps, which was understandable given her upbringing, but certainly not some wilting flower that could be easily manipulated. Seemed to me she had leverage. All she had to do was threaten to tell Alison about her husband's affair and his stolen jewelry business. Maybe she did, and maybe Alison didn't believe her—or care.

Or why didn't Catherine go to her father? After all, Franklin was Kalen's boss. She could have gotten Kalen fired. But that might have made things worse for her, put more pressure on her from Kalen with the stones. I could see why she felt she had to extricate herself from under Kalen's thumb first. And she had no real proof of where these stones were coming from. Kalen could have claimed he'd had them for many years.

I wasn't going to be able to let this go. I needed to talk to Catherine, even if it meant losing her as a friend and tenant. Even if the police didn't think the displaced pin was strange, I did. And if they did decide it was strange, they would come looking for Rose or Catherine. Whoever was responsible for putting this amber-colored pin in Rose's display case would give us the answer to this murder. Who killed Kalen, and why would they move the pin?

I paid the tab for breakfast at the register and left for the Mill. I figured Catherine would be there; she often worked on Saturdays. But I shuddered at the thought of going back into Montgomery Mannequins.

The door to Rose's Vintage Dresses was open as I came out of the elevator on the second floor. Of course Rose wasn't there. She was at the hotel; this was the last day of her show. I glanced at the glass étagère. The pin was still there. I heard Catherine moving around in the back.

"Hi, Catherine" I called out loudly.

Catherine was working at her workbench as if it were any other day, her back to the door. "C'mon in, Laney," she called over her shoulder. There were stones and beads all over the workbench. Brilliant glass ones and elaborate ceramic ones. Many were loose and some were still in their original settings. Three sectioned trays held crystals, beads, and findings, and there were several tools scattered around. Catherine looked like a miner with her headlamp on. She was closing a jump ring on a bracelet with two pairs of needle-nose jewelers' pliers.

"Catherine, I told Dale—Detective Adams—this morning about the topaz pin I found back here in Rose's cabinet. He'll have someone come by, probably soon."

"Hello?" A deep voice from the front door of Rose's shop made us both jump. We turned in time to see an officer in a blue uniform standing up front in Rose's doorway.

Quickly I whispered to Catherine, "Looks like they didn't waste any time. I'll see you later."

Murder Among the Mannequins

"No, wait. Stay," she commanded, adding, "please?"

The officer, whose name badge did indeed say Thurgood, as Dale had promised at breakfast, proceeded toward us. He looked from me to Catherine and said, "Catherine Gilbert-Smith?"

"That's me," she said in a determined voice. He handed Catherine a search warrant for the pin. After she read the paper, Catherine led him back up to the front door and opened the display case. The officer pulled a latex glove on his left hand and gingerly placed the pin in a small paper envelope marked "Evidence."

They exchanged a few words, of which I heard "… need you to come down to the station with me. We'll need to talk to you some more and take your fingerprints."

"I'll finish up here and come by this afternoon." Catherine's face was stoic but pale as she came back to her workshop.

"Look, you have a lot to handle right now," I said. "Is there anything I can do?" She slumped down on the couch. Her stoicism had left.

"I don't know what to do." She looked beaten.

I looked at her, waiting. I was beginning to wonder if she was more involved than I thought. Was I ready to defend a guilty person because I liked her? Suddenly I didn't know which side of the fence I should be on. I needed to give this some space to think about it. When she remained silent, I left and walked down the hall to my studio.

The gold script on the door of Montgomery Mannequins was still obscured by crime scene tape. My stomach did a flip-flop. The body. I

133

pictured the blood soaked into the floor. I was glad there would be no working in there today. I started back to the elevator, where Catherine was waiting.

She was full out crying, but I managed to make out between sobs, "I need to tell someone . . . I should never have done it. I need to know what to do."

Chapter 21

I needed to hear Catherine out. I felt like I at least owed her this. We walked back into her workshop, to the couch. She was shaking, and I wanted her to sit down before I had to catch her.

"So why did you do it?" I'd leave it to her to decide which to tell me about—the jewelry fencing or the murder.

Then she began to speak slowly, pausing between each sentence, gulping great breaths of air.

"The truth is, when I spent that semester in Italy, Kalen wasn't just my neighbor. We had an affair—just a fling, really. I figured I was in Italy, I'd never see this person again. As you know, after I finished college, I went to work for my father's company, Gilbert Strickland. Some years later, whom should he hire but Kalen Farrell! He was okay at first. We were cordial, but then he started making noises about seeing me again. Lots of overtures, unwanted ones. By this time, I knew a lot more about him. He was married, and he had been when we were in Italy, a little detail he had hidden from me, and I knew he wasn't the sort of person I wanted to be involved with.

"I was feeling pressured. I wanted to get away from Kalen, or at least stop him somehow. I told him I would tell his wife, not only about us, but about the stolen jewelry too. He just laughed! The bastard! He said

Alison knew about us already, and as long as he didn't leave her, she didn't care. He said she'd never believe me about the jewelry fencing … after all, why did he need money? He had married into her family's wealth."

Catherine paused, then added "And then I knew he'd never leave her family name and money, so my leverage dissolved."

"Why *did* he do it? The fencing, I mean."

"It was a power thing with him. He used to brag about how it felt to be making money so easily off of others. He saw it as a win-win situation. His clients got money—a pittance from him, plus the value of the jewelry from their insurance companies—all while keeping it secret from their friends. He got all the profit from turning over the stones. It's not like it was costing him anything to have them reset!" she scoffed.

Catherine began to quietly cry again. "That's what I was doing— by resetting the stones, I was erasing any trail of stolen gems that led to Kalen! And then he said, 'Do you think I would risk everything I've achieved just for you? Maybe for the jewelry, but not for you!' The bastard!"

Tears were pouring down her cheeks by now. If she was trying to manipulate me, she was good.

"I can't believe you got pulled into this, Catherine." I shook my head.

"Finally I told him I'm out of his scheming. By then, I didn't care what it would cost me, even my reputation."

"So why didn't you follow through?"

She paused and pursed her lips. "Sit down. It gets worse."

I sat and waited, wondering what else could be coming.

"Kalen told me that my father was embezzling money from his own clients."

"What!?" It sounded preposterous.

"Yeah, I just laughed at him when he said that. My father is the most honest person I know. And why would he undermine his own company? It's just ridiculous." She paused and looked as if in deep thought.

I took a breath and searched for something to say, but my thoughts were interrupted.

"Kalen showed me statements that recorded money being transferred from their clients' accounts into my father's personal account. And he was ready to leak that information to the press if I didn't shut up and keep setting the stones for him."

"But why would your father risk going to jail? Why would he risk losing his clients and undermining his own company? That doesn't make sense."

"Exactly. I didn't believe Kalen at first when he told me. But Laney, the statements don't lie."

"How do you know Kalen didn't fake them just to blackmail you?"

She closed her eyes and leaned against the back of the couch, as if considering this. "Well, I don't, really. I'm sorry to pull you into this, Laney. It's not your problem." She was as limp as a rag doll.

From what I had learned about him since his death, I realized the list of those who wouldn't mind seeing him dead was growing. I was afraid the police would stop at Catherine and not look any further, and I just couldn't accept that she was capable of murder. Now I was more determined than ever to figure this out. Damn Kalen! He was the one who'd pulled me into this by getting himself killed in my studio. If Kalen didn't fake the statements, why would Franklin embezzle from his clients? I mentally ticked things off. Kalen was blackmailing Catherine over the affair and being an accessory to stolen property. Maybe Kalen was blackmailing Franklin too, once he discovered Franklin was embezzling. Maybe Alison was getting tired of his womanizing and his underhanded schemes and was ready for him to be gone. After all, what did she really need him for? The more I learned about him, the more motives were surfacing, and the more I disliked him.

"I think you should have another look at those records of your father's, Catherine." Once we discovered whether Franklin was embezzling or not, it would perhaps answer one question. "Maybe it's not as it looks. There has to be another explanation. Do you have access to them?"

"Well, I do have keys to his office from when I worked there last summer, but I don't like snooping around." She searched in her desk drawer for the keys.

"Think of it as defending your father," I reasoned. In the same breath I added, "I'll go with you." I was determined to get to the bottom of that bastard Kalen dying in my studio and implicating my friends and me.

I let her think about this as I started to gather up my purse and jacket. Maybe I could check on my studio while I was here. Really, the last thing I felt like doing was going back in there. I wondered if the crime lab was finished yet. By now maybe Elise would have called for a cleaning service and the place would be back to normal. At least on the surface.

"Laney!" A booming voice jolted me and I looked up, surprised to see Dale in the doorway. He looked as surprised to see me. Behind him, the faces of Thurgood and Bradford were beginning to look entirely too familiar.

"Catherine Gilbert-Smith, we'd like you to come in for questioning about the death of Kalen Farrell." Dale spoke fast, and louder than was necessary since we were both within his arm's reach.

"What's going on?" I suddenly felt defensive of Catherine.

He didn't answer me, just looked at me with a professional, albeit none-of-your-business, look. But my presence didn't stop him from telling Catherine, "We have more questions for you. We'd like you to come down to the station now. Laney, you'll have to come down sometime and give us your fingerprints too."

"That's ridiculous!" I spluttered.

Thurgood informed me, "We have to check yours and your mother's too. Burl's too, for that matter.

Dale placed a hand on Catherine's arm. Where did he think she was going to go? There was no back door.

Catherine's face was turning red, but I couldn't tell if it was anger, rage, or frustration. I was feeling all of those.

"Of course my fingerprints will be on the sword!" she shouted. "I repaired it and set the jewels for Laney." Her face registered my own thoughts. *You idiots!* But her face registered fear too.

"It's best if you come with me. Now." He steered her toward the door.

With a frantic look, Catherine tossed her keys to me. "Please, Laney, you'll have to do it! *Pronto!*"

Chapter 22

*D*ale hustled Catherine out into the hallway, calling over his shoulder, "I don't know what Catherine was referring to, but Laney, keep out of this." His warning tone just fueled my determination.

I ran out after them and stood staring as they marched her into the elevator. I leaned against the wall. Too much was happening too fast, and I was having trouble sorting things out. I didn't know what Catherine meant either. I forced my brain to blank out for a moment. I was glad it was Saturday and I wouldn't have to set foot in my studio for a few days.

I needed to clear this up, not only to clear my head, but I was getting angrier that they seemed to already think Catherine was guilty. I looked at the keys in my hand and realized that's what Catherine meant. I wondered if they would get me into the Gilbert Strickland building, or just Franklin's office. *There's only one way to find out*, I thought, and walked slowly toward the stairwell. I wanted to give the cops a head start out of the building. Better for them not to see me leaving on their heels.

On the first floor, I came across Howard and Carlos standing at the front door, watching Catherine climb in the police car and the car leave the parking lot.

"What's happening?" Howard had sad eyes.

"They want to question Catherine about the death of Kalen Farrell."

"Oh no! She couldn't have done something so awful!"

I shot him a look. "I know. It's just ridiculous," I called over my shoulder as I left the building.

The Gilbert Strickland Building sits on the corner of Light and Fillmore in the heart of Baltimore's financial district, several blocks north of the newly renovated tourist and nightspots at the Inner Harbor. The old architecture was still impressive. The columns and cornices spoke of an era when Baltimore was a wealthy port city. Most of the buildings in this section of town had been designated historic landmarks, and so kept their ancient, preserved facades.

I pulled into the parking garage across Fillmore Street from the Gilbert Strickland building. It was pretty empty this morning, being one of several garages around the Inner Harbor mostly used by the weekday nine-to-fivers. It was too early for tourists and shoppers. I parked near the exit door of the garage, nose out, in case I had to beat a hasty retreat. My stomach was tying itself in knots. I realized I hadn't eaten in a long while. I needed fortification. A block away was a Starbucks, and while I wasn't a big fan, I figured the hearty coffee would be just what I needed. And a pastry wouldn't hurt. I sat at their window seat and calmed my nerves while I polished off the chocolate croissant and half of my coffee.

Snapping the lid on, I wedged the cup into my bag.

Murder Among the Mannequins

Across the street, the massive glass doors of the Gilbert Strickland building were standing open to the lobby. Inside was a man studying the directory on the wall next to the elevator. I tried to look like I belonged there, and at the same time hoped he wouldn't ask me for directions. I'd have to confess I was a stranger to the building.

I was relieved that the elevator was waiting on the ground floor. I hurried inside and pushed the "close doors" button while the man was still busy at the directory.

When the doors opened on the top floor, I stepped out and panicked when I saw a maintenance worker swabbing the floor at the far end of the hall. I ducked back in the elevator as he turned at the sound. I held my breath and slowly counted to five, then peeked around the corner of the elevator door. He had returned to his work. I stepped out and squeezed behind a potted plant. It was large, but not large enough to hide me entirely. The maintenance man rolled his cart into a door and closed it behind him.

There was only one door with a sign on it, which I assumed meant the entire floor was dedicated to Gilbert Strickland. I tried first one key, then another, until I was in. I told myself that the keys in my hand gave me permission to be here, and wondered if this was still breaking and entering.

Inside, there was a receptionist's desk in the corner of the room, and nothing else. The desk was clear of anything but a nameplate and an elaborate telephone system. It could have been a movie set, devoid of anything personal. Ahead, there was a long hallway with several doors leading off of it.

I started with the first door. I tried the only other key on the ring, but it didn't fit. Great, I'd have to try every door along the hallway. I had an idea. I skipped the next two doors and went to the last one, figuring the boss would have a corner office. The key fit smoothly.

The door barely cleared the thick carpeting. I looked around at a room full of ergonomic executive furniture in dark cherry, a real executive office that was so devoid of anything personal that it, too, could have been for a movie set. There were windows along two walls, meeting in the corner, offering a panoramic view of the city. The other two walls were lined with floor-to-ceiling cabinet doors of rich cherry wood. In the center was a large, elegantly carved wooden desk. It held a large leather desk blotter with matching notepaper holder and penholder. The only other thing on the desk was a sleek telephone resting in its base.

I closed the door gently behind me, placed my bag on the desk, and began opening cabinets, looking for a computer. The first cabinet yielded a shelf full of top-shelf liquor, Chivas Regal and Glenlivet, and a shelf of crystal drink glasses. The cabinet below disguised a small refrigerator. The next cabinet was locked. Finally, in the corner cabinet I found a computer and slide-out keyboard.

I pulled the chair from the desk in the center of the room across the thick Berber carpet. I was breathing heavily, my heart racing. Was anyone else working in the building today? What if that janitor was intending to clean all the offices? I switched the computer on and the realization

144

that I should be wearing gloves made me feel like I was truly doing something wrong. Snooping around had a steep learning curve, a model of trial and error, which I did not intend to pursue after today. While waiting for the computer to boot up, I looked behind the other cabinet doors.

Wow. Some office! Besides a second mini refrigerator, a flat-screen TV, a stereo, and a stack of CDs and vinyl, the next three locked doors suggested perhaps file cabinets. I ran my fingers across the warm cherry wood of the massive desk in the center of the room, then quickly thought better of it and buffed away my fingerprints with my sleeve.

"Password," said a voice behind me. I jumped and turned around to see the computer had a blue screen with a blinking cursor.

I slid into the chair and stared blankly at the screen. It blinked back at me.

"Password," the voice said again. I frantically looked for the low volume button. The last thing I needed was for that worker to find me here and call his boss—or worse yet, the police.

Password? Even if I knew the password, there was no place to type it. I sat there thinking. Suddenly a window popped up on the screen with a dialog box to fill in the password, and a flashing cursor nagged at me again. I was surprised he didn't have a faster computer.

Okay, I'll take a stab at it. Nothing to lose, I thought.

I typed in F-R-A-N-K-L-I-N. Denied.

I tried again. C-A-T-H-E-R-I-N-E. Denied. Then I typed in the one I should have thought of first: G-I-A, Catherine's mother. A dialog box popped up telling me I had one more chance before it locked me out.

Damn! I wondered if it was tied to a silent alarm if I gave the wrong password.

The password. What could it be? Had Catherine told me? But she didn't have time. I thought back to the scene in her workshop. She had tossed me the keys. What had she said? 'You'll have to do it! *Pronto.*'

I held my breath and mentally prepared to vacate the premises quickly if this didn't work.

I typed in P-R-O-N-T-O. Bingo! I was in.

Chapter 23

I breathed again. I didn't know what I was looking for, but I was pretty sure I'd know it when I saw it. Fortunately, Franklin was a very orderly person. His office *and* his computer screen were spartan. Besides two application icons, there were only three folders on the screen. Much as I wanted to snoop in the one marked "Personal," I skipped to the one called "Financial Reports MFS."

I opened the first folder. The files were listed alphabetically. I quickly sorted by date. I felt overwhelmed. Just what *was* I looking for? Withdrawals, that's what. I opened the first file in the list, saw that it was thirty pages, and decided it was too lengthy to print. I scanned the list for a shorter file, hoping for a summary report of some type. The third file listed was a weekly summary. Great!

Somewhere down the hallway a bell rang. I froze, straining my ear. It was the elevator outside the front office. Then the front office door opened and I held my breath, listening for footsteps, but heard nothing except a door closing up the hall. And then the building was quiet again. I had to get out of there before whoever had come up to this floor found me in Franklin's office. I quickly commanded the computer to print in draft mode, hoping it would print faster and quieter than my own printer.

I grabbed the papers from the printer tray and stuffed them into my bag, knocking the lid off my coffee, and my bag off the desk. *Damn!* The coffee spread to a circle, half of it under the desk. There was no time to hunt for towels or cleaning supplies. I snatched my scarf from around my neck and mopped up as much of the coffee as I could, trying not to spread the stain any larger. I stuffed the soggy scarf into my soggy bag and turned off the computer, quietly closed the cabinet doors, and looked around Franklin's office to make sure there was no other evidence I'd been there.

I cracked open the door and peeked out. There was no one in the hallway; I quietly closed and locked Franklin's door behind me. If someone was in his or her office down the hall, I couldn't risk summoning the elevator. There must be a stairwell somewhere. The exit sign above the door across from Franklin's office proved to be an entry into a stairwell. I made it down four flights without breathing much and without much noise. The lobby was empty, and I bolted out into the fresh air and sunlight. I felt like a thief who'd gotten away scot-free. Then the realization hit me; I *was* a thief who'd gotten away! I started a brain war again: I was not a thief, I had a key. But I didn't have permission. Yes I did, just not Franklin's.

There was more foot traffic now. I lowered my face and moved quickly to the garage. It had filled up significantly since I'd parked. I was anxious to get away, so I took the shortest route out of the city. Unfortunately, I hit every red light between the parking garage and the highway. I kept checking the rear view mirror, and sped up once I got onto 395. Ten minutes down the road, as I was finally beginning to relax, I saw flashing lights in my rearview mirror. *Damn it. Did I trip a silent alarm in Franklin's office?* I prayed that the police car would pass me and pull over the car in front of me, but as I slowed down and pulled onto the shoulder, so did he.

I tried to look innocent; I gave a feeble smile, kept my hands on the wheel, and asked the officer what the problem was.

"Do you know how fast you were going?"

"No, sir, but by the look on your face, I can only guess I was going over the speed limit." I could feel the beads of perspiration on my forehead, and hoped he didn't notice. Once he took my license and registration back to his car, he took his time writing out a ticket. I tapped out a rhythm on the steering wheel and rubbed my arms to ward off the chill I felt. What was taking so long?

He was back beside my window and handed me a ticket. "You were doing sixty-eight in a fifty-five. Watch your speed from now on, ma'am." I let out a sigh. It was the first time I was relieved to get a speeding ticket. I was still shaking, but I stayed under the speed limit the rest of the way home, still checking the mirror every few minutes.

In the kitchen, I grabbed a granola bar and spread out the report on the kitchen table. I was glad Elise was out running her errands. The more I read, the less I understood. It was obvious I needed help. I thought for a moment. Not Rose; I needed math help. Catherine was out of the picture. Mary-Taylor! I quickly called my fellow Quilt Tart.

"Hiya. What are you doing?" I tried to sound casual.

"Right now?"

"Yes."

"I'm working on that new quilt we talked about for the guy in Rehoboth Beach. Why?"

"I need help. I have a financial report that I'm trying to make sense of."

"For your company?

"No, this is for something else. I have a weekly log in front of me. What I'm really looking for is a discrepancy, something that doesn't add up."

"I can't help you on the phone. I'd have to see it. How about tomorrow afternoon?"

"How about today?"

"Sounds urgent, Laney. Okay, I'll meet you at Annie's in twenty minutes."

"No, I'd rather do it here at my house."

Mary-Taylor barely paused, then said, "I'm on my way."

Chapter 24

*M*ary-Taylor showed up twenty minutes later with her eight-year-old daughter, Molly, in tow. I squinted at the noontime sun reflecting off her glasses as she came in the front door. Her short, blond bob whipped around her face. She looked the picture of preppiness in her skinny jeans and pink Henley sweater. It seemed ironic that such a tiny five-foot-one, size four person should have such a mouthful of a name. She had told me how other kids used to call her MT, which had morphed into "Empty." So I always made it a point to use her full name, mouthful or not.

"Molly, would you like to take Jesse outside? Her ball is in the backyard. And there's a jar of dog biscuits on the kitchen counter."

"Sure!" Her eyebrows went up. "Okay, Mom?"

"Okay. Just stay in the backyard."

Mary-Taylor went directly to the kitchen table and started looking at the papers I handed her. She straightened up after studying the report. She adjusted her glasses. "I'm not sure what you're looking for, but I don't see anything wrong. Of course, what you have is only a snapshot."

"What do you mean?"

"Well, this is a weekly report of transactions. There's nothing to compare to, or add up. It shows which accounts took money out and which ones put money in, and when. It indicates heavier transactions on Monday and Friday than the other days that week, but that's not unusual. What you really need is the monthly or yearly report if you want to see the big picture."

" Oh, of course. I guess I'll have to go back." I sounded as annoyed as I felt.

"Back where? Laney, what's this about? It looks like privileged information. I'm not sure I should be looking at it. And I'm not sure I want to know how you got it." She checked on Molly out the kitchen window.

I stood up and paced the kitchen. I had to tell her the whole story. "Catherine Gilbert-Smith was picked up this morning for questioning about the murder."

"Murder? What murder?" It took her a moment to place Catherine's name. "Isn't Catherine the young woman who shares Rose's shop?"

"Yes. She's at the police station right now for questioning. Kalen Farrell was found dead yesterday in my studio." Then I hesitated a moment. I didn't know if, or how well, she knew Kalen. How should I describe him? Catherine's business acquaintance? Friend? Lover? Father's employee?

I said simply, "Kalen was an acquaintance of Catherine's who supplied her with some of the stones she used in her jewelry, and he worked for her father's company." Both things were true. Best to leave it at that.

"And these reports have something to do with the murder?"

"Well, they might. They might provide evidence that someone else had a motive for killing Kalen, besides Catherine." No need to bring Franklin's possible involvement into this yet. I just wanted to deflect suspicion away from Catherine, but onto whom I didn't know.

"Catherine gave me the key to Franklin's office and told me her father's computer password and asked me to have a look at his financial records. I figured it was important to her. And it's the only way I can help her right now." I tried to be sufficiently vague, knowing I'd have to fill her in on the details of Catherine's suspicions of embezzlement soon.

"Well, you need more information than this report gives. Can you get a monthly statement, or at least several weeks' worth of summaries?"

"I guess I can print out everything in the statements folder." My stomach churned at the thought of going back there, especially for long enough to print out reams of information.

"No, you don't need that much. You said you have a key, right? I'll go with you. I might be able to zero in on something useful. But you've got to clue me in to what you're looking for. I figure you must have a good reason."

I wanted to wait until it got dark to attempt another trip to Franklin's office, so while Mary-Taylor left to take Molly shopping for school clothes and then get her situated with her favorite sitter, I forced myself to walk Jesse around the property and heated up leftovers for dinner.

Mary-Taylor showed up again at 6:00 p.m.

"Come on, get in. I'll drive."

I didn't think I looked as tired as I felt, but I was glad to climb in the passenger side. We made it downtown in fifteen minutes, a record by any standard. The sun was setting now, but it would have been a good day for an Orioles game; bright and sunny, had they not been playing away this weekend. I tried to slow my nonstop chattering, a habit that I knew gave away my nervousness. Still, I talked about the sports season and the neighborhoods we were passing, noting the houses and yards becoming increasingly smaller the closer we got to downtown. Still, there was evidence that folks were taking care of their houses: raking and doing other chores, reminding me that I could have been doing the same this afternoon. Or at least checking in with Ted about the lawn and rose garden. I tried to think of anything except where we were headed and what we were doing.

I directed Mary-Taylor to the same garage I'd parked in before. We crossed against the light to the Gilbert Strickland building. The lobby doors were locked this time, but I pulled out Franklin's keys and found the one I needed. This time there was no one in the lobby. I didn't realize I was holding my breath until I exhaled loudly. Nervous as I was, I was feeling more at ease breaking into Franklin's office for the second time, though that realization didn't make me feel any better. The elevator doors opened and exposed a maintenance worker polishing the walls. *Damn!* It was the same man I saw before. I busied myself with rummaging around in my purse, burying my face as much as possible, and trying to stall.

Mary-Taylor breezed past me and stepped into the elevator.

I reluctantly got in. We chattered the whole time with small talk, purposefully not punching the fourth floor button until the worker got off on the second floor. I was trying to appear more relaxed than I was feeling. Once again, Franklin's key let me in, and I opened the corner cabinet, pulled out the computer keyboard tray, and entered the password. I accessed the directory of accounts in the computer quickly this time.

Mary-Taylor pulled over a chair and immediately opened the large file that I had skipped earlier and began scanning the transactions. I looked over her shoulder, but her fingers flew over the keys so fast I couldn't follow her. I paced the carpeted floor. What if that workman came up here? I walked to the door and listened. I peeked out. Nothing.

It took Mary-Taylor only a few moments to find something that made her say "Ahh. This is the file you want, Laney." The printer started humming away, sounding loud in the quiet room. I jumped and put my hands on the machine, trying to quiet it, much like I did with the old washing machine at Elise's.

"There's a pattern here." Leave it to a quilter, especially one who's a math whiz, to spot a pattern. Mary-Taylor pointed to a column of numbers on the screen and quickly scanned down several pages. She seemed unconcerned with the noise of the printer.

"What do you mean?"

"Look at the weekly picture here," she explained. "There are lots of withdrawals, which are then deposited back into the same accounts about three days later. That in itself is not too unusual, I guess. Most are Fridays and Mondays," she added, glancing at the calendar on her phone, "but look at the times of the entries. These times are automatically recorded when each transaction is made."

I scanned the columns.

Most of the entries on the screen were during normal business hours, and were under a couple of hundred dollars each. But there were more than a few whose sums were larger. Much larger. They were each posted late in the day, seven, eight o'clock, like someone was working overtime. I whistled softly.

"About this time," I said, looking at my watch. Suddenly, I felt more uncomfortable being there, even though it was Saturday. "Let's get out of here." I jumped up and grabbed my purse.

"Not so fast." She reached out and tethered my arm. "Look at this. All the withdrawals between, uh," she said, running her finger down the column, "eight forty-five and nine p.m. on the seventh of last month totaled"—she did a quick tally—"$4,992,000."

Five million dollars! On one day! I was having trouble wrapping my brain around that.

Mary-Taylor sorted the withdrawal column by dollar amount. Most transactions were in the several-hundred to several-thousand-dollar range—maybe enough to repair a roof on one of those Roland Park homes, or tide you over till your CD matured. Then there was a huge jump in the dollar amounts as I scanned down the column. The next entry was $189,995.00! The next eleven transactions were large and on the same date. She hit another button and the information jumped to another

order—by date. There was another batch of high-end transactions every week or so. She paged down to the end. All the high ones were around $200K, and there must have been a hundred of them.

Mary-Taylor double-clicked on each line and stared intently at the screen as the dialog boxes popped up. "Laney! They were all transferred into the same account number, and then transferred back into their original accounts three days later." Her voice was barely above a whisper, but I could hear the urgency in it.

She pointed to the screen. "See, each transaction dated three days later totals the exact same amount, and were time stamped between 7:15 and 7:30 p.m. Three days later would have been a Monday. This is more than coincidence, Laney. What if one person made all these transactions?"

"And did what with it? They put the money back into the same accounts! That in itself doesn't make sense. And where would they have put it if they had kept it? You can't walk around with that much money in a suitcase!"

My brain was fried, but I could see Mary-Taylor intensely scanning all the transactions, double-clicking on each withdrawal, and scribbling down something.

"I think I have something. Laney, look here." She pointed to the dialog box that popped open. It showed a lot of numbers that didn't mean anything to me.

"The money was transferred into this account. See?" She pointed to the first few digits of a long stream of numbers. "This is the SWIFT code, and these are the bank routing numbers followed by the account number receiving the money. Every one of these large transfers has the same deposit numbers."

"What's a swift code?" I asked, trying to follow her.

"Stands for Society for Worldwide Interbank Financial Telecommunication. It means the money went to a foreign bank. The next number is the routing number, the ID for the specific bank or brokerage house, and notice that all these high-value transactions are to the same bank, and the same account!

With a few lightning-speed keystrokes, she tried to access the information for that account. A warning dialog box popped up on the screen that read "Secure Account. You do not have authorization to access this account."

"Weird!" I said. "How can Franklin be denied access to something on his own server? Unless ... he doesn't know about it."

"Okay, now it's time to go," Mary-Taylor said, her voice shaking.

I dove for the printer. This time I had come prepared with a briefcase, which I filled. Mary-Taylor stood up but continued to give the computer commands. I hoped she was returning the file to the state we had found it and was erasing any trace that we'd been there. She turned off the computer and closed the cabinet.

Just as I reached for the doorknob, the door swung toward me, cracking my knuckles. I jumped and screamed and found myself face to face with Michael Leland.

Chapter 25

*T*his was the first time I had seen Michael since meeting him at Annie's over lunch on Wednesday. He looked the same, only those warm brown eyes weren't so warm this time.

"Laney?!" Michael sounded as surprised as I felt.

"Michael!" *Oh damn, what if he was the one doing this embezzling or whatever this was?* I knew we had to talk our way out of here, and quickly.

There was a long pause. Somehow, I felt like *he* owed *me* an explanation. It took me a moment to realize it was the other way around.

I started babbling. "You heard Catherine was arrested for Kalen's murder, didn't you?" This wasn't exactly true, but I was trying to distract him from any more questions about our presence, which was like trying to hide a twelve-foot beach ball.

"What? That's ridiculous! What are *you* doing *here*?" He wouldn't be swayed from the beach ball.

"Catherine gave me the key. She asked me to get some information for her," I said indignantly. "Mary-Taylor"—I waved toward her—"was helping me." I hoped he would accept this vague and shallow explanation.

He hesitated for a moment, and then pointed at a chair, nodding for me to sit. I perched on the edge of the seat.

"What kind of information?" he said to us both, but he was looking at me.

"Reports." Okay, so we were dancing around the real issue. But maybe he was the bad guy here. How did I know how much I could tell him? I just needed a way out, fast.

"Okay, Laney, I see you don't want to tell me, but this *is* Franklin's office, and you *are* here without his permission, even though you *say* Catherine gave you a key. Now do you want to tell me what's going on?"

Somehow, I couldn't see Michael as the perpetrator. I didn't have a choice not to trust him, even though it might get me in hotter water.

"Catherine wanted to check out a series of large withdrawals," I said, euphemizing what she had told me. "She was about to look into it when the police came to talk to her."

Michael was silent for a moment. He stroked his chin. "How does Catherine know about any of this?"

"She was informed that large sums of money were being withdrawn routinely. But since she was taken down to the police station for questioning about the sword, she asked me to look into it."

"Who told her that? "

"She didn't say." I still didn't know for sure if Michael was in on this, and I wanted to keep the pool of suspects as wide open as possible.

"Look, we both know that something isn't right here," I confessed. "I'm just trying to help Catherine." I stood and picked up my bags: my purse and the briefcase that hopefully contained evidence that would lead us to whoever was behind this. "She's afraid someone is framing Franklin. I'm trusting it isn't you. And I'm telling you it isn't Catherine. I brought Mary-Taylor in to help sort this stuff out." Mary-Taylor was standing frozen next to the computer. I decided to not involve her any more than I already had, which was a lot.

Michael briefly shifted his eyes to Mary-Taylor, and returned them to bore through me.

I took the lead. "So if this isn't your normal work schedule, why are *you* here?"

"I don't owe you an explanation, Laney." His shoulders relaxed a little, and then he offered, "But I'm doing the same thing as you. Although I'd rather be home tearing out the walls in my den. Anything else you want to know?" I detected a little sarcasm in his voice.

"No, I think we found what Catherine wanted and we just need to get it to her."

"I think you've done enough, Laney. Franklin and I are on top of it. Catherine needs to talk to her father. And *you* need to leave it alone!" Where had I heard that before?

Oh! Catherine! I needed to find out if she had been arrested. I dialed Dale's number. I doubted the precinct would give me any information, but I knew he would be able to get the details.

"Hello?" Dale answered on the first ring.

"Hey. Can you do me a favor?"

"Anything."

I had a fleeting appreciation for Dale's willingness to do anything for me.

"Find out if Catherine Gilbert-Smith has been arrested or is out on bail or is being held overnight at the station. Can she have visitors? I need to know what's going on."

"Give me a minute. I'll call you back."

Just as I hung up, my phone buzzed. I didn't recognize the number, but I answered anyway.

"Laney, can you come get me?" It was Catherine. "They've said I can go. I need to get out of here. I don't want to call Father; he would send the car, and I just need to see a friendly face."

"Sure. I'll be there in fifteen minutes," I said, and hung up before realizing I had not driven here and didn't have my car.

Chapter 26

"Oh, damn. I just told Catherine I'd come get her, forgetting that I didn't have my car here, Mary-Taylor. I don't want to keep you; I know you have to get home to Molly."

"I'll get Catherine and take her home, Laney," Michael offered.

"No, I want to tell her what we found, since she asked me to do the sleuthing. I'll call Uber."

"That's foolish. We'll get her together, and then I'll take you home." Michael's eyes were warm again.

Part of me leapt at the thought of being with Michael, but part of me saw flashing warning lights. I still didn't know who was behind all of this. In the meantime, I texted Dale that I had already heard from Catherine.

Catherine was waiting outside the precinct when we pulled up.

"What a nightmare! I never want to go through that again." I could hear the anger and frustration in Catherine's voice on top of the weariness, and now surprise. "Michael, what are you doing here?" She looked at him, then at me, brows furrowed.

"I hope you didn't say anything to them," Michael interjected.

"They already know about Kalen's gems being real. They questioned me about that."

"What? What gems? Catherine! Didn't you call Bernard before you said anything?" By the anger and intensity of his question, I surmised that Bernard was the Gilbert-Smiths' lawyer.

"I didn't think I needed Bernard!" Her shoulders slumped even more. "So now they still think I'm their strongest suspect. They said they don't have any others. They gave me the old 'Don't leave town' order."

"If they don't have any other suspects, it's only because they don't know Kalen!" I said. Knowing what Catherine had told me about him, I could imagine there were a lot of people who wanted Kalen dead. His wife Alison for one, and maybe even Franklin. I just had to prove it.

"Laney, you've done so much for me already. I can't ask anything more." She let out a sigh. "Just take me to my car at the mill please, Michael."

"Catherine, you need to talk to your father, and the sooner the better."

There was no way I was leaving this hanging. I handed her my briefcase and filled her in on the evening's events, and the conclusion that Mary-Taylor and I had come to that something fishy *was* going on at Gilbert Strickland. But not instigated by Franklin, if he was denied access to the foreign deposit account.

"Michael's right, Catherine. You need to talk to your father."

She sighed again, and I saw tears welling up in her eyes when I glanced back at her.

"I'm just so tired of all this."

I seized on the moment. "So let's go right now." I glanced at Michael to see if he was game.

Michael nodded, already making a U-turn. "Good idea. We can get your car later, Catherine."

"I know you've had a rough couple of days with Kalen's murder in your studio, Laney. You don't need to be involved with our other problems too."

"I'm not sure I have a choice." It was nagging at me; these two things were too coincidental. I didn't like coincidences.

Michael didn't need directions to Franklin's house; he turned uptown toward the Guilford neighborhood of the city while Catherine read over the papers Mary-Taylor had printed out.

"Oh God, I'm afraid Kalen was right. There's a clear pattern of money moving in and out of these accounts. You got this from my father's computer?" Catherine sounded as forlorn as she looked.

"Yes. And it doesn't make sense that people would have pulled money out and returned it within a few days. So many of them. And such large amounts. It's just odd." It was quiet in the car as I thought about everything. "And when Mary-Taylor tried to trace the transactions, she found they were all going to the same account with an international routing number. When she tried to get into that account, we found that account was locked."

"Oh, this doesn't sound good." Catherine wiped her eyes with the back of her hand. "I've read about 'blind accounts,' but I never came across any when I worked there."

"And that's not all. Something Mary-Taylor noticed was that there were no large transactions, either out or in, since last week. Prior to that there was a large transaction of some sort every couple of days.

"How come you're here, Michael?" asked Catherine.

I could finally laugh about it. "We were about to leave when Michael showed up and scared the crap out of us. He thought we were behind it, and we thought he was." I was turned around in my seat and mouthed to Catherine, "Still not sure he isn't."

"So I showed him the key you gave me so he wouldn't think we broke in, and . . . well, it took some convincing, but I think he knows we're on the right side of this. Do you know if anyone else besides your father can access his personal files?"

"I don't know; I wouldn't think so." She stared out the window, where the gray skies made the quiet day even more silent. The homes were becoming increasingly larger, and more expensively landscaped and better kept than the homes in the center of the city. Michael turned onto a small side road in Guilford and pulled into the driveway of a good-sized house, though small by this neighborhood's standards. The house was ablaze with lights and looked inviting.

Catherine mounted the front steps and rang the doorbell. I was surprised she didn't have keys to her parents' house, but then I realized her keys were back at the mill. I could hear the Westminster chimes echoing through the front hallway as the door opened.

"Hello, Mother."

Giovanna was just as I remembered her from the one time she had stopped by Catherine's shop: a tall, stately woman with silver hair pulled into a French roll. I was surprised to see her opening the door. I would have thought everyone in this neighborhood had house staff.

"Caterina! What a nice surprise." She wrapped her arms around Catherine. Her voice was soft, and she had more than a trace of her native Italian dialect.

"Well, come in, come in," she said, stepping back and opening the door wider.

"Hello, Laney. It's nice to see you." I was surprised she remembered me. She did not wait for a response from me.

"And Michael! Is Franklin expecting you?" She had a puzzled look on her face, but quickly recovered her composure. "Come in, all of you, please." She stepped back to let us in and gestured toward the first room.

We were ushered into a formal room to the right of the hallway. Most of these grand old homes had a front parlor. This one was no exception. The room had a huge, but worn, Oriental rug the size of the entire room, and was filled with antiques. Their warm patinas told me that Giovanna had never had to buy furniture; these antiques had been in the family for generations.

On the way into the parlor, I whispered to Catherine, "Do you want your mother to hear this too?" She seemed to be the gatekeeper to Franklin.

"Might as well. This affects the whole family."

"Please have a seat," Giovanna said to us, offering us the sofa and sitting down in the wing chair.

"Would you like something to drink?" Apparently Giovanna wasn't one to let manners slip; she spoke in a calm, slow voice, unlike what I was feeling. A small, thin woman appeared in the doorway. She was in street clothes, not a uniform, but she waited for instructions. I hadn't even noticed Giovanna beckon her.

"A ginger ale for me please, Eileen. What would you girls like? Michael?"

"Ginger ale is fine," Catherine and I said at the same time.

"Nothing for me, thanks, Giovanna. We really came to speak to Franklin."

"Thank you, Eileen," Giovanna dismissed the maid. She had a kind way with the help, unlike some employers.

Catherine avoided the issue of the strange money transactions and instead broke it to her mother that Kalen was found dead at the mill.

"I know. His wife called us yesterday. What happened? A heart attack?"

"Not exactly," I responded to her question. "I found him yesterday. He'd been killed with a sword from one of our figures."

"Dio mio! Murdered? Oh, Alison didn't give us details. And you found him? How terrible for you."

Catherine mentioned calmly that the police had been talking to her along with everyone else at the mill. She made it sound casual, like she was one of many. I knew differently. I let the two talk while my eyes wandered around the room. The deep crown molding emphasized the high ceiling. The drapes were not new, but were obviously custom-made of heavy silk shantung. The wallpaper was a large and busy print, not to my liking, but it suited the room. Michael was shifting from one foot to the other, but let Giovanna speak.

"Catherine was just filling me in on what she asked you to do," Giovanna retrieved my attention.

She seemed unfazed by my snooping around in Franklin's office, so I was beginning to feel less guilty. She stood and walked to the doorway, where Eileen stood with a tray of our drinks. She handed them to us.

"Yes," she said slowly, looking from Catherine to me to Michael. "I think it's time you talked to Franklin."

Chapter 27

*G*iovanna disappeared down the hall. I wasn't sure she meant for us to follow. Catherine stood up, yet waited for her mother's return. Giovanna reappeared in the doorway, her posture ramrod straight.

"Franklin's in his study. Please follow me." She spoke in such a calm voice I wondered if anything fazed her.

Franklin's study was remarkably similar to his downtown office. The wood paneling and furniture was the same rich cherry, but Giovanna's softening touches were evident here. There were oil paintings on the two side walls and tapestry pillows on a comfortable-looking couch. I could tell at a glance this was not the fake stuff off a bolt, but real tapestry, the scenes woven in deep, rich colors. The floor was covered with another room-sized Oriental rug. Ahead, the large windows looked out over a garden that would be shady even on a sunny day, lined with massive boxwoods and huge ivy-covered trees. The fountain showcased an angel whose vessel was chipped and dry; it looked like it had been keeping watch for many decades.

Michael took a seat in one of the leather wing chairs against the wall. He seemed to be enjoying my discomfort.

Franklin spoke first. "Thank you, Gia." He indicated for her to move to his side.

I stepped forward to take his offered hand when Giovanna introduced me.

There was a long silence. I felt that I owed him an explanation of how I came to be standing in his study, but I waited to let him or Michael begin. I sure didn't want to tell this man, this icon of the financial world, that somebody was fiddling around with his clients' money. Especially if it was him. I looked toward the door. I felt like I did the first time I went skiing: standing at the top of the tallest mountain in the world (it was the bunny slope), I desperately wanted to be somewhere—anywhere—else. *There's only one way out of this*, I had told myself, and pushed off down the hill. Now, I took a deep breath, and started off.

"Mr. Gilbert-Smith, I—"

"Papa," Catherine interrupted, putting her hand on my arm, "you know I love you, and would never do anything to hurt you." She inhaled deeply and continued while Franklin waited.

She cleared her throat and squared her shoulders.

"Papa, it's come to my attention that the company might be in some trouble." I wondered if they were always so formal in their speech to each other. It had sounded so soft and natural when Gia had spoken. Now it sounded like a business transaction.

Catherine handed him the report. I was happy to let Franklin think that Catherine was the one to go into his office. I'd rather not implicate myself, and I was thankful that Michael had not reported seeing me there, let alone Mary-Taylor, who was only there at my insistence.

Franklin interrupted her, reaching for, but not looking at, the papers. "I know what you've found. I've been aware of this for some time now."

"You have?" Catherine and I spoke at the same time.

His voice gained a hard edge to it. "But first, why were you in my office? Especially after hours? Why didn't you just come to me, *cara*?" Catherine filled him in on Kalen's suspicion that money was going missing and his ridiculous claim that it might be Franklin's doing.

"So Kalen knew about these transactions? And he didn't come to us? He came to you?" Franklin and Michael exchanged glances.

"Yes, Papa, but I knew that couldn't be true. I wanted to figure this out before coming to you with Kalen's outrageous story." Catherine's face was flushed and she looked at the floor. I knew what she was feeling since I felt it too; how could we even half believe that her father would sabotage his own company?

I decided to come clean and get out from under this cloud I was feeling.

"Mr. Gilbert-Smith . . ." I began.

"Please, call me Franklin."

I was honored, even though I felt awkward using his first name. He was always "Gilbert-Smith" in the newspapers.

"Franklin,"—it sounded strange coming from my lips—"we were just trying to get to the bottom of this before we came to you." I felt heat rising in my face. "We even thought it might be Michael."

"Michael?" Franklin laughed and glanced at Michael, sitting in the side chair. He seemed to be enjoying this. "What made you think Michael was involved?"

"Well, he came into the office while we were there, and it was the same timing as those transactions . . ." Oops. I was the one who slipped, so I just came clean. I told Franklin how Catherine gave me his office key and computer password right before she was taken in to the station for questioning, how she asked me to look at the statements showing the large sums of money being moved around, and how Michael came in and caught me red-handed, so to speak.

Franklin chuckled gently.

"No, I can assure you that it's not Michael. He and I have been working on this together for the past few weeks."

"Oh, Papa! What's going on?" Catherine's shoulders were still tensed.

"Sit down, Catherine, Laney," he commanded in a kind voice. He turned to look out the window at the garden, his back to us. We sank into the leather chairs in front of his desk. Giovanna hadn't moved from Franklin's side. Franklin gestured for Michael to join him.

"First of all, everything I tell you is privileged information." He looked pointedly at me. "Nothing leaves this office." I nodded.

"Michael discovered the pattern a few weeks back." Franklin turned to face his desk, and across it, us. "It's not unusual for our clients to move significant sums around," Franklin said without hubris, "but there were too many of them, too evenly spaced, too routine. And we discovered that the deposits were being put into a blind account, just as you did. I asked Michael to override the system to get the identity of the account holder." He turned from his desk and walked back to the window.

"So, who is it?" I asked. I was in for a pound by this time.

"Me." His voice was calm.

Giovanna turned from the opposite window to look at her husband. They looked like two bookends, perfectly framing Franklin's many awards and certificates on the wall between the windows.

"That is, it has my name on the account," Franklin continued. "The routing number indicates it's a foreign entity." He paused and then answered our unspoken question, "Of course I didn't set up the account."

"And international laws being what they are, we're having trouble finding out who did, unless we bring a criminal suit. Michael's been going into the firm at off hours to investigate. We're trying to solve this without involving the courts and the media. Especially the media. If this got out, it would devastate us."

Franklin reached for Giovanna's hand. His voice was now as soft and smooth as aged bourbon. "Cara Gia, this is why I've been so preoccupied. But telling you the whole story only would have worried you, and that wouldn't help matters."

Giovanna's face remained stoic, but showing concern for ... what? For Franklin? For the company? For the family's reputation? Disappointment in his not confiding in her?

He dropped her hand and turned to me. "Laney, I'm sorry Catherine involved you in this. I hope we can trust you to keep this information confidential," he reiterated. "Michael and I will handle it from here." His eyes bore the seriousness of his message, but I wasn't ready to let it go. I couldn't shake the feeling that this might have something to do with Kalen's death.

Chapter 28

*W*e left Catherine with her parents, and when Michael pulled into the driveway of RoseHaven, I realized I didn't recall anything of the drive home. It was a silent ride, my mind trying to piece together the information Franklin had given us.

I entered my quarters through the back door, intending to make a quiet entry. But Jesse announced my arrival with her typical jumping and barking.

"Laney? Where've you been all day?" Elise called from the kitchen. I groaned. This was another of those times I felt pushed to look for my own place.

"I spent it talking with Catherine." Well, that much was true, and I didn't intend to fill her in on any more details.

"You know you should leave it to the police! Why do you feel compelled to put yourself in the middle of a murder investigation? Leave it alone!" She gave a disgusted sigh.

I didn't answer and she stopped pushing.

I let Jesse out to run for a few minutes, and stood staring out the back door. The day had ended as badly as it had started. I was tired, and I was looking forward to having another day before facing what I now thought of as a crime scene instead of my office. I drifted off to sleep, wondering if they had gotten the blood out of Grandpa Albert's old wooden floor.

The next morning was Sunday, and I was more than ready for a slow day with no plans. I woke up around nine with Jesse nuzzling my face. I had a nagging headache. It was overcast, so I let Jesse out the back door to make her daily rounds without me and put on some coffee. Elise had left a note on the kitchen table saying, "Going to the office to make sure the crime scene cleaners have been there. Spending the rest of the day with Howard—checking out fixtures for the restaurant."

I welcomed a day to myself. I was glad Michael and Franklin were taking over one of Catherine's problems, though something about it was still bothering me. I just didn't know what. I paced the kitchen while the coffee was brewing. My head was buzzing with all that had happened yesterday. I welcomed the quiet house so I could try to make sense of things.

Catherine certainly had motive for wanting to get rid of Kalen. So did Franklin and Michael, since their investigation was narrowing down the source of ... what? Money laundering? Borrowing funds? Just what was that money swapping all about? That part still puzzled me. Could Giovanna have known about Kalen's pressuring her daughter to work with stolen gems? Or even Catherine's affair with Kalen? Could she be protecting her husband's—and her—reputation, both the business's name and their family name?

I poured coffee into my favorite mug, the one Molly had made for me in summer camp, laced it with cream and sugar, and sat down at the kitchen table.

Michael had the least motive for getting rid of Kalen; I sure didn't know him well, but it seemed highly unlikely he would risk his future for Franklin's reputation. Or even the company's. What else was Kalen into? Repurposing gems, either stolen from Kirkland Fine Jewelry or fenced for his elderly clients, possibly screwing with clients' money for what reason I couldn't understand, his affair in the past with Catherine. He had mentioned real estate when I first met him at Annie's. Buying up old buildings to rehab them. Could he have been Carlos's and Burl's landlord that jacked up the rents and effectually dumped them out on the street? Bad enough Carlos lost his studio, but Burl lost his housing. I could see where that might make someone angry, but angry enough to kill?

What about Kalen's wife? Did Alison know about his philandering? How many "other women" had Kalen had? What if Alison found out he was stealing from Kirkland Jewelry, *if* he was? The spouse is always a suspect, right?

And who could have gotten into Montgomery Mannequins without breaking in? Plenty of other people had access into the mill building: Howard, Rico, Bea, Mary-Taylor, Carlos, even Ansel, plus any number of customers for any one of us, not to mention the front door being left open a lot recently. And why was someone after Rose's dresses? Why in the hotel and not her shop?

I let Jesse in the kitchen door once I realized she was outside, whining to come in. I poured some kibble into her bowl and refreshed her water. I had to let this go for now. I took advantage of Elise being out and fried up an egg and some bacon.

In the late afternoon, Howard and Elise came back, chattering about the state-of-the-art commercial kitchen appliances they'd seen. They hauled in five bags of groceries from various markets. I was getting used to Howard being there, cooking up a storm with Elise. Soon the house smelled of wonderful aromas, but it didn't stir my hunger. I told Elise I would skip dinner and retreated to my quarters with Jesse, closed the door, and curled up on the bed. I put on a movie, hoping it would give me something else to think about. Unfortunately, all it did was put me to sleep and into a dream about someone in a dark hoodie running after Kalen with a sword, yelling, "Stop! Stop!"

Monday morning I stepped out of the mill's elevator, relieved the yellow tape was gone. Elise was already in the office, and I was glad for the company there. I dropped my jacket and bag at my desk and opened the back door from the office into the clean room, where Kalen had lain. The bloodstain was still there, seeped into the old hardwood. I closed the door again. I'd rather enter the now-ironic "clean room" by way of the storage area. This morning I needed to focus on Miss Prudence and her torn dress. By now, Rose was back from the bridal show, and this was a repair I could do today, while she had new customers to attend to. I brushed off the large worktable, laid the dress out, pulled up a stool, and gathered my hand-sewing supplies. This needed to be a nearly invisible repair; the pin, once replaced, would cover the small seam that would be visible. After a while I looked up and massaged my throbbing temples. The clock said it was nearly noon. It was a good time for a break.

"Mom, Burl, I'm going out for lunch. Do you want me to bring you anything?" I called out.

"None for me, thanks," called Burl.

"No, thanks, I brought in leftovers. There's enough for you if you'd like some."

It was tempting. Elise's leftovers were always good.

"Thanks, but I've got to get out of here for a while."

I threw on my jacket and turned up Washington Street, heading for Annie's Tavern. For once, I thought walking was a good idea. I needed to clear my mind. All morning something about the Prudence figure had been nagging at me. Why did her dress get torn? Why not just unpin the pin? And I still couldn't figure out how, or why, the pin got into Rose's shop.

As I stared down at the patches in the old sidewalk, I tried to connect Kalen's murder to the torn dress and the pin. Why would a murderer steal the pin from one place but return it somewhere else? And who would know where to return it? Catherine, Rose, I ticked off my fingers; I guess anyone who had heard about the pin. That included Kalen and Michael at Annie's on Wednesday.

Annie's was filled with the lunch regulars. I knew what I wanted without looking at the menu. A shrimp salad on white toast with extra

180

mayo to go. Shellfish was one of my comfort foods. I gave my order to Cindy at the counter. While I waited, I caught Annie's eye across the room and waved. Annie gave her customary nod as she delivered lunch to a man sitting alone with his back to me. I realized it was Michael. My heart started pounding as I quickly turned away from him. I remembered our last uncomfortable meeting at Gilbert Strickland. But then I recalled Franklin's reassuring words and his kindness to deliver me home, and figured it was as good a time as any to talk to him.

"Laney, that'll be nine fifty. Need anything to drink?" Cindy brought my attention back.

"Uh, no."

I paid for my lunch, then took the bag over to Michael's table.

"Hello, Michael, mind if I join you?" He looked up with a mouthful, and I sat down on a chair opposite him, not waiting for a response. He lifted his eyebrows quizzically as I unwrapped my sandwich and took a bite.

"Hey, Laney," Annie, too, greeted me with a puzzled look as she refilled Michael's coffee cup.

"Hi, Annie, could you bring me a cup of coffee too? Looks like I'm eating in," I mumbled with my mouth full.

I waited until Annie left. "Any more news? Did you and Franklin find out anything for certain?"

"Nothing. Things have been quiet on that front."

"I'm glad I bumped into you. I feel bad about the other day."

"Bad about what?"

"That we thought you were the embezzler."

Michael actually smiled. "As long as we're confessing, I thought you or your friend Mary-Anne might be involved. After all, you were there in the wrong place at the wrong time, or the right place at the right time, as it were."

"Mary-Taylor," I corrected him.

"Yeah, her."

"Is there any way of finding who set up the account?"

"Nope. Foreign laws are very protective of account holders. That's why I've been going in evenings. As much as anything, I thought I might just get lucky and catch the culprit red-handed. Assuming he, or she, is doing it from the company turf."

"Any luck?"

"Yes and no. I never caught anyone, but I did find something that confirms our suspicions."

"What's that?"

"I think someone else has solved our problem for us. You noticed the pattern of transactions?"

"Yes, many large withdrawals and deposits on one date and the reverse two days later."

"So you noticed there were no large withdrawals last week?"

"Yeah. But what does that mean?"

Michael finished his sandwich. He looked pensive as he pushed his empty plate away from him. "Let's go for a walk."

Chapter 29

I tossed my bag and empty coffee cup in the trashcan on the way out the door. Outside, we headed south and walked past the mill, turning east toward Canton Riverside Park.

"Franklin and I noticed the pattern of transactions several weeks ago, as we told you. We realized that it would be devastating to not only Gilbert Strickland's reputation, but to Franklin, personally, if it became public. Before we involved the police, we wanted to give ourselves time to find out who was behind it." We walked silently for a while.

"And?" I prompted.

"Our network is set up so that every account rep can get into his own clients' accounts, but not into the master file. This blind account we found was opened under Franklin's access code, which means someone besides Franklin or myself had gotten into the master level using Franklin's code."

So far, I was following him, but I was puzzled.

"Why would someone go to the trouble of setting up a phony account just to transfer money into it and right back out to the rightful owners? Seems like a lot of trouble for nothing."

"Oh, it may look like nothing, but Laney, you've got to look at the numbers."

I waited for him to explain. We reached the park and sat on a bench at the far edge. The wind had picked up and was tossing leaves around my ankles. I tugged on my socks, trying to close the gap between them and my jeans.

Michael continued. "On the surface, the only damage it was doing was stealing a couple of cents of interest from the client, right?"

"Right." That much I could follow. "So what's the big deal? Find out who it is and fire him."

"Laney, five million dollars at five and a half percent is seven hundred fifty-four dollars. Per day."

"What would pay five and a half percent?" I didn't know a lot about investments but that sounded ridiculously high in this economy. My savings account only paid half of one percent.

"Well, it would have to be a foreign equity or bond, but a very risky one. Probably what we call a junk bond."

It took a minute to sink in. "You mean, he—or she—was making roughly fifteen hundred dollars every weekend for twenty minutes' work?"

Michael nodded. "Times thirty weeks. And that's all we know about so far."

"Not bad." I was impressed with the brains, and gall, of said perpetrator. Borrow someone's money, not too much from any one person, and not for too long. Not in cash, which would be easy to detect, but into junk bonds. Not long enough for them to notice unless they scrutinized their statements daily. My guess was most people who had their money with Gilbert Strickland didn't.

"But it's so easy to do!" I looked out over the water, thinking about what Michael had just told me.

"Easy maybe, once you're set up. But very, very risky. There's a chance the bond would lose money in those particular two days. Not to mention, it's illegal and could land you in jail."

He continued in a low voice.

"Everything was pointing to Kalen, but we have no proof. He worked late hours. His clients were mostly elderly wealthy women; he didn't bring in many young people. If his clients called when he was out, they would always say they would wait for him rather than talk to another rep. I think he sweet-talked the women, the older and richer, the better.

"One day, one of our clients called up, irate because Kalen was supposed to move around a couple of thousand dollars between her accounts and it didn't show up for three days. Caused her all kinds of embarrassment. When I asked Kalen about the transaction, he pointed out it had been a weekend and a bank holiday, and assured us he would smooth it over with the client. So we let it go."

Michael shook his head. "Hindsight!" he spat out.

"It wasn't until one of our most wealthy clients, Mrs. Edmund Munroe, called demanding to speak to Franklin. Her accountant had spotted some movements in her account that 'just didn't look right,' as she said. When she couldn't answer his questions, saying she hadn't moved any money around, and certainly not that large an amount, she called Franklin. She was furious, demanded an explanation.

"So that's when Franklin and I went over the books with a fine-tooth comb. We always have our accountants do spot checks on all the reps' accounts, but spot checks had revealed nothing out of the ordinary. But once we looked at the details over the longer term, the first thing I noticed was that many of Kalen's accounts had much more activity than anyone else's, and they seemed too consistent. You know we frown on that at Gilbert Strickland, making commissions on unnecessary transactions at the expense of our clients."

That was not something I ever thought of, and it made me think that I needed to pay better attention to my own financial future. Mannequins and quilts alone weren't going to carry me through old age.

"We were trying to catch the person red-handed so we had something concrete to discreetly hand over to the police. This morning when we noticed there had been no large transactions this week, we thought the problem might have solved itself."

I looked at Michael. "You think that's proof that Kalen was behind it?" My thoughts trailed off.

" . . . And Gilbert Strickland's problem could either die a quiet death"—I realized—"Or . . . it could give you and Franklin a motive for Kalen's murder." I looked up at Michael. Somehow, I didn't think I was sitting on a park bench with a murderer. On the other hand, money could make people do some really strange things.

"How close are you to Catherine?" It was an unexpected question from Michael.

"Not close, really."

"So how did you get involved in this?"

"Michael, you wouldn't believe it." I shook my head. "It all started with a pin."

I related to him in a nutshell the whole story of the mill as a haven for artists, getting to know Rose, and subsequently Catherine. How Rose's dresses came to be used on my figures, and Catherine's pins on Rose's dresses. How I was the lucky one who found a dead body among the mannequins in my studio, how Miss Prudence's pin was ripped from its dress, and how it showed up in Rose's shop. I told him how Catherine pleaded with me to help her as she was being carted off to the police station. What I didn't tell him about was Catherine's affair with Kalen, his stolen-gems business, and her unwitting involvement. My head was spinning by the time I finished, but Michael digested all this as quickly as I said it.

"You know"—he kicked at the grass with his shoe—"Kalen has been with Gilbert Strickland for three years. He came in after his wife's family sold their jewelry business to a conglomerate."

"I thought Kirkland Jewelry was doing well. Everyone knows Kirkland Jewelry."

Michael frowned. "That's what they want everything to think, but the truth is, the profits had dwindled, and her father had to sell it. The buyer wanted to keep the name. So from the outside, everyone thinks it's still owned by the Kirklands."

"That would explain the need for money, all right."

"Franklin had known Kalen for years, and I think he offered him the job more out of sympathy than anything else. But Kalen was a fast learner, and he was a smooth talker, especially with the older ladies. They loved him. And, to his credit, he did well for them. His client base grew with all their referrals, and his numbers looked good at the end of every month, so Franklin was pleased."

He emitted a sort of grunt. "His base was 90 percent women. Most all were older and widowed." He paused. "He always was a ladies' man, so that in itself didn't raise any flags."

"So you know about his affair with Catherine." I blurted it out before I had time to think.

He looked up suddenly. "Catherine? Don't you mean Giovanna?"

"Giovanna?! No, I mean Catherine," I said a little too loudly. A bird fluttered out of a nearby tree. I was beginning to feel sick. Having affairs with both mother and daughter? Ew.

We sat in silence, staring at each other, trying to comprehend.

Michael enlightened me. "I overheard Kalen on the phone one day. He had put it on speakerphone. It was late, and I'm sure he thought everyone was gone. I heard a woman's voice telling him to 'leave her alone or you will regret it' and 'using her like you used me all those years ago.' It was Giovanna's voice, I'm sure, and she was really angry. I knew

Kalen had spent some years in Italy, but I learned a long time ago to keep my nose out of other people's personal lives."

I shook my head to mask the shudder I felt coming on. "I knew there was something I didn't like about him. He just seemed too slick when I met him. Nothing specific I could put my finger on at the time, though."

This new information gave me something to think about. If it was Giovanna on the phone that day, what if Catherine knew about Kalen's affair with her mother? Would it give her more reason to kill him? Could Giovanna have been angry enough to kill Kalen to protect her daughter? If she knew about the stolen jewelry, it would add fuel to her anger. It was all too much.

I sat back on the park bench. Suddenly, I was very, very sorry I had let myself get dragged into this whole sordid mess. It seemed to be consuming all my thoughts when I had other problems looming on the horizon, namely my mother and her damn restaurant.

Chapter 30

*I*t was early afternoon when I got back to the studio. Miss Prudence was finished, with the exception of the pin, and I didn't know when, or if, I was going to get that back. I couldn't think about that now. I'd have to ship her off to her new home with a temporary pin and have a reproduction made.

I returned several calls and caught up on the mail. There were requests for bids on several new jobs, but I didn't have the mental clarity to tackle those today. I spent the next couple of hours housecleaning my desk and the rest of the office, with the exception of Elise's desk. I needed some order in my life. Two hours later, I felt a little better and decided to call it a day. I thought of Elise banging pots and pans around in the kitchen and realized with a jolt that I was like my mother in that regard—organizing my surroundings when life was chaotic around me.

Jesse was eagerly pacing when I walked in the door at RoseHaven. She was still a puppy at heart, and hopped around whenever anyone showed up. I let her out the back and watched as she took off on her usual route past the carriage house and down the old, rutted driveway through the woods.

The house was quiet, but I smelled the lingering aroma of herbs and garlic. Elise was beginning to keep irregular hours at the studio, spending more and more time on the restaurant.

I sighed. Another thing I didn't want to think about now.

I decided to make use of the remaining bit of daylight and grabbed a novel from my reading table. I took the pillow from my wingback chair outside to the lawn beyond the kitchen door. Elise refused to add a deck since it wasn't historically accurate to the architecture of the house, but we had carved out a nice flat spot between the kitchen door and the rose garden. Ted had done a nice job of adding shrubs and annuals around the short, lush grass. It had much more character than a deck. The waning sun felt good on my face, and the wind was tempered in this protected nook.

My mind kept wandering, so that I found myself on page ten and didn't know what had happened so far in the story. I closed my eyes and let the book slide to the ground as the sun warmed my face.

Voices coming from the kitchen woke me with a start. I could hear Elise discussing the merits of vitreous china with someone. It must be Howard, I thought.

The wind had picked up and the sun was nearly down. I shivered, gathered my book and pillow, and went in the kitchen door. I realized that I'd really miss these aromas here once the restaurant materialized. Jeez, I'd have to go to the restaurant to get a home-cooked meal.

"Laney, I wondered where you were. I parked behind your car. Will you need to get out?"

"Hi, Howard. No, I'm in for the night."

"What's for dinner?" I asked Elise. She definitely seemed to be taking the lead in launching their new project. I could see Howard's value was as her sous-chef. Perhaps he'd be happy to stay in the kitchen cleaning up, but Elise would have to be out greeting the patrons.

"I thought I'd work on my Maryland Crab Imperial recipe."

"M-m-m." I sat down at the kitchen table. Sure, I'd miss these dinners, but on the other hand, it'd be easier to lose those ten pounds I was battling.

Howard was standing at the counter, picking through the crabmeat for shell. He made quick work of it and began pulling sour cream and salad greens out of the refrigerator. Their conversation centered around food, of course, and I pulled out a paper napkin from the basket on the table and began doodling. Jesse gave up whining and sat at Howard's feet, waiting for him to drop something—anything other than the dry food I had put in her bowl.

I pulled out several more napkins and lined up a row of three, then added a second row underneath. The miscellaneous colors of the napkins were beginning to take shape as a quilt. I added a third row to form a square, a nine-patch in the quilt world.

I wrote Catherine's name on the corner of the first napkin and drew a line diagonally under it, from corner to corner, dividing the square into two triangles. In the bottom triangle under Catherine's name, I listed "affair, stolen jewels, blackmail?" as her motive. On the second napkin, I wrote Giovanna's name, and again divided it into two triangles with my pen. Under Giovanna's name, I wrote "affair (s)? & husband's financial scandal." When had she found out about Kalen's stealing from Franklin and possibly trying to ruin his reputation? Had she known about it before Franklin told us in his study? I stared off into mid-space. Nothing was as it seemed.

Elise was mixing crabmeat with Hellmann's mayonnaise, sour cream, and a dab of Dijon mustard in a large mixing bowl. Howard was washing out the crab shells to hold the concoction to broil when it was done. Jesse remained fixed at his feet, occasionally scanning the floor.

I sat back. Franklin and Michael had pinned down Kalen as the likely culprit of the illegal financial transactions, but would Franklin have resorted to murder to protect his company? Would Michael? I wrote Franklin's name on the third napkin and Michael's on the napkin that started the second row, and put "save company" under Franklin's name. I tapped the pencil on my head. I added "affairs" under Franklin, in case he knew about either of them. I couldn't think of a motive for Michael, so I crossed off his name. For now.

Alison! She might want to be rid of Kalen for a number of reasons. I penciled her in on the first napkin of the second row in place of Michael. Under her name, I wrote "K's affairs, stealing from Kirkland?"

Who else had a grudge against Kalen? Maybe more people than I realized, given all the things I had learned about him in the last few days. Well then, who had access into the mill? The front door was always locked, especially overnight. All the tenants had a key to the front door. Some routinely worked at night, so there may have been someone the police hadn't questioned yet. But then I remembered the day I found the door propped open. Granted, that was in the middle of the day, but someone could have left it open when they left for the day. I couldn't rule out the possibility.

I closed my eyes and thought back to who might have gotten into my studio without breaking in. Elise, Burl, and I were the only ones who had keys to our studio. Would Burl have killed over someone trying to steal a pin? Had he caught someone trying to steal something in his workroom? What was this thing that he had against his old landlord, and was that Kalen? I had to be objective, and reluctantly put Burl's name in the center block with "had access" under it. I added "motive??"

Something was nagging at me. How did someone, or some ones, get in to Montgomery Mannequins two times without forced entry? They must have had a key. But no one else had a key to Montgomery Mannequins, did they? None of the tenants would have been given a key. Not even Howard, with his close ties to Elise. Even so, Howard, like the others, had access to the front door of building, so I gave him his own square at the end of the second row of napkins, but added "motive??'" the same as in Burl's square. I sat back and looked at the two rows of names and the row of blank napkins underneath.

I had to write Carlos's name on the napkin that started the third row, with "access to mill" and "lost studio because of Kalen?" in the lower corner. Bea and Mary-Taylor had keys to the front door of the building. I filled in the third row of blocks with their names, so that all nine blocks were filled. All of these people had access, at least to the building, if not our studio. Bea and Mary-Taylor had no motive that I could see. Bea had ready access to wholesale gems, so I discounted her killing for the pin, and besides, it wasn't really stolen; it was found in Rose's shop. On the other hand, she alone would have recognized the value of the topaz, but I doubted if that was enough to kill for.

I shook my head. What was I thinking? Bea and Mary-Taylor were my friends! My "objectivity" was beginning to scare me. I crossed their names off. I knew them too well. They couldn't kill anyone. Except perhaps in self-defense. And they wouldn't have done it in my studio. And they would have told me about it.

But what did I know about Rico? He had access into the mill, not that he ever came in much. I had heard him encouraging Catherine's Italian several times. I remembered her saying she had met him briefly a long time ago. Did she know him from her time in Italy with Kalen? Did he know about Catherine's troubles with Kalen? Seemed far-fetched, but I wrote his name in the bottom row on the middle napkin. I left the last napkin blank. Then I thought of Ansel. He seemed to show up at the weirdest times and places. I wrote his name in the last square. His only possible attachment to the crime was, as far as I could tell, "shows up everywhere and creeps me out." So that's what I wrote under his name on the last napkin. Weak, I know, but I couldn't dismiss him just yet.

I sat back and stared at the patchwork of colors, names, and words on the table. It looked like a quilt that was almost, but not quite, finished. The quilt top was there, but it sat as an unfinished project. I pulled over the basket that held the remaining napkins and set it on top of the paper quilt. I stood up, poured myself a glass of merlot, and looked out the back door to clear my head. Outside, the winds were picking up, pulling leaves off the trees and layering them in the rose garden. Elise was setting the table in the dining room and chatting over her shoulder to Howard, this time about colors to paint the main dining room of the restaurant. Howard had come into the kitchen to toss the salad.

I couldn't shake the thought of someone leaving a body in *my* studio. I felt like my space, my building, had been violated. I was surprised to realize that it wasn't Kalen's death that bothered me as much as the fact that someone had gotten into our studio and left the detritus for us to discover and deal with. That included the broken mannequins and the questions with loose ends, as well as the bloodstain on the floor. I was also surprised at my possessiveness of the company, the one I couldn't wait to leave behind in order to spend time with the Quilt Tarts. Hmmm. Maybe that figure of me was having an effect. I'd deal with that later.

Chapter 31

I walked back to the kitchen table and lifted the basket to look at the colorful layout of napkins. I rescued a wayward piece of lettuce that Howard had tossed outside of the bowl and munched on it absentmindedly.

The first block was Catherine's. Of course she had access to the building, and she had a pretty strong motive when I thought of the affair, the stolen gems, and the overall bullying of Kalen toward her. Plus, she may have found out about his affair with her mother years ago. I really didn't want to ask her about that. But I couldn't see her as capable of murder, especially leaving him in my studio. She would have had more access to Kalen outside the mill. I turned her napkin facedown.

The next two blocks contained Giovanna and Franklin. While they both had motive enough—Dale had told me stories of homicides for less—they didn't have access into the building, much less the studio. Either of them would have had easier access to Kalen outside of the mill. I crossed through their names and then flipped each napkin facedown to reveal its blank side.

The second row contained Alison. Ditto for her: of course she would have killed him in their home or his work, or anywhere else rather than the mill. Unless she wanted to frame Elise or me. Or Burl. But why?

We really didn't know her, but maybe that was her plan. To direct suspicion onto someone unconnected to her. I had to leave her name faceup.

The next block, the center of the nine-patch, listed Burl. Yes, he had access to the studio, as did Elise and I, but motive? Still, I couldn't cross him off just yet. There was that thing with Carlos and the unknown landlord, and I didn't know how deep that went, or even what it was about. Which led to Howard on the next napkin. Access to the building, yes, but motive? For now, I left Burl and Howard faceup also.

The bottom row of napkins read Carlos, Rico, and Ansel, all of whom could get into the building, but not easily into Montgomery Mannequins. I grabbed my head. It was beginning to throb, whether from thinking or from lack of food, I couldn't be sure.

"Is dinner ready yet?" I called into the dining room.

"Come and sit down," Elise answered. "We're already eating. Didn't you hear me call you?"

"Sorry, no." I set the napkin basket again on top of my paper quilt, took my place in the dining room, and dug into the Crab Imperial. For once, I was glad that the conversation centered on the restaurant. That left me with my own thoughts. I glanced up to find Howard and Elise looking at me. I hoped they didn't think me unsociable, but I had my brain wrapped around this thing and I was having trouble letting go of it, even though the Crab Imperial was superb.

"More wine anyone?" asked Howard. He retreated to the kitchen for a refill.

"No, thanks." The first glass wasn't doing much to dull the throbbing of my head.

He brought the dessert in with him—a huge cranberry compote with whipped cream. That was another good thing about their new interest—they made commercial-size quantities, so that even the leftovers in this house were to die for.

I exercised every ounce of willpower I had and excused myself without dessert. At least my head was beginning to feel better. I rinsed my dishes, placed them in the dishwasher, and returned to the puzzle of napkins and names on the kitchen table. I moved the basket to the side to block Elise and Howard's view. I already knew Elise's opinion of my sleuthing. I didn't want another lecture, and I didn't want to answer any questions about my paper quilt.

The remaining six faceup blocks read Alison, Burl, Howard, Carlos, Rico, and Ansel. Alison may have had plenty of motives, but she had no access to the mill, and obviously had more access to Kalen outside the mill. I turned her napkin facedown. I studied the possible motives of the remaining five. Burl and Carlos's tiff seemed to be that, a disagreement between artists. Nothing to do with Kalen. Wait, didn't Kalen say last week at lunch that he was buying up real estate? What if he was the one dumping all these artists out on the street? But that didn't seem a strong enough motive for murder. I knew Burl and knew he was levelheaded, so I turned his square facedown. But I didn't know Carlos well. I studied the remaining names on the paper quilt: Carlos, Howard, Rico, and Ansel. But what could have been a strong enough motive for any of them to kill Kalen? And how did any of them get in to Montgomery Mannequins?

The key ring! On the security guard figure outside our door! That was the secret to finding the killer. I needed to check out that key ring.

Suddenly, the hair on the back of my neck stood up. I grabbed the napkins off the table and stuffed them in my pocket. How could I have not seen this? I stood up slowly and put my wine glass in the sink. I glanced in at Elise and Howard to see them now looking over a folder I knew housed their notes on the restaurant. That is, Elise was looking in the folder, her dinner plate now pushed to the side. Howard was cleaning and stacking the dinner plates. Always cleaning up! They wouldn't miss me.

I went into my bedroom, picked up my keys from the desk, and went quietly out the back door of my room.

"Stay, Jesse," I whispered as she sat down and looked up at me quizzically. I closed the door gently. My thoughts were swirling. No, could it be? I should have seen the signs. But I needed proof.

I walked around the back of the house to the side where I had parked. Howard's car was behind mine, blocking me in. I got in and slowly steered my car straight ahead past the house and down the old dirt driveway. The trees soon swallowed up my car. The old tire ruts were overgrown with weeds but I could follow Jesse's trail. I hoped the cracking of the fallen leaves and sticks I was running over was not as loud as it sounded to me. I emerged from the woods onto Hartmann Avenue, turned left up the hill and passed the paved driveway. I glanced at the house and was reassured that all was still quiet.

Murder Among the Mannequins

I turned right onto Chandler Street and drove downtown. The mill's parking lot was empty. The clouded moon shed little light on the front door. Once in the darkened building, I used my phone's flashlight. I didn't want to call attention to being in the mill. I didn't want to risk the elevator acting up, so I took the steps and entered Montgomery Mannequins's office to pick up the master key Elise kept in her desk. We both always made a point of respecting the tenants' privacy, and didn't use this key unless in an emergency. But if this didn't qualify as an emergency, I don't know what did.

Outside our door, I passed Chester, the security guard figure, where I stopped to inspect his key ring, again kicking myself that I hadn't followed through on Elise's suggestion to sort through them last week. The spare key to Montgomery Mannequins was not there. In fact, the entire key ring wasn't there!

"*Damn!*" I voiced my surprise to the empty hallway. Where was the key ring? I hadn't noticed it was missing before this. I decided to give a cursory look into the other studios.

I found my way to the stairwell and went down to the first floor, still using my phone's light. I made it to Rico's door and fumbled with the key. Once inside, I turned on the lights. There were sheets of metal and rods and bars stacked everywhere. There was not a single horizontal surface clear. A welding machine took up the only empty space. I walked around it, looking for anywhere he could have hung or tossed a key ring. Nothing obvious here. I turned out the light and locked the door. Across the hall, I unlocked Carlos's door. Inside, it was fairly spartan. Shelves full of cameras, tripods, and albums. A sink with nearby cabinets of chemicals. A large-screen computer. No key ring.

I hurried back toward the stairwell and climbed the flight to the third floor, avoiding the steps I knew to be creaky. I was pretty sure the mill was empty, but my nerves were telling me to be aware. I was still using my flashlight. At Howard's studio door, I paused again to listen for any sounds in the building. It was quiet. It took some jiggling to get the master key to turn in the lock. The hinge and the floor creaked simultaneously as I stepped inside and closed the door behind me. I fumbled for the wall switch, and a vast brightness flooded the entire room. The last time I was in this studio was before Howard moved in. Now it looked more like an art gallery than a working studio. The door led into a small hallway enclosed by white gallery walls, which stopped at a seven-foot height and opened above to the twelve-foot ceiling. Each wall along the hallway held a long row of paintings. Each had a predominant color different from the surrounding paintings. It looked like a rainbow of primitive art, not like any of his paintings I'd seen before. I looked closely. Each held his trademark signature across the bottom.

The hallway opened into a spacious room with white walls. In the middle of the floor were two easels that stood side by side with their backs toward me, supporting one large canvas, which bisected the room into two areas, art gallery in front of me and working studio beyond. Behind the large painting, a small wall cabinet spilled supplies out onto the table below it. Then I saw it! The key ring lay on the counter amidst a pile of paint tubes. I continued my surveillance of the large room, riveted to one spot in the center of the floor and pivoting to take it all in. I felt sick to my stomach. I'm not sure what I expected, but it wasn't this. Catherine's face peered at me from every angle, and in every color. Her face filled one canvas; the next depicted her resting on a chaise, the typical "fainting couch" pose. I slowly moved around the room, passing Catherine's image time after time, until I got to the back corner. The floor was spotless, hardly the typical floor of an artist. I turned to face the large painting in the center of the room. A plastic tarp protected the floor under the oversized canvas. Here was the only work-in-progress in the room. I wasn't surprised to see it was of Catherine, in full color and larger than life. In fact, at this point, I would have been surprised if it had been of anything else.

My hair was standing up on the back of my neck and I felt goose bumps on my arms. I had to get out of there. I had seen enough.

As I stepped around the wall that made up the front entry hall, I gasped. Howard was standing at the other end, blocking the only door out of the studio.

Chapter 32

"I was afraid you'd figured it out when you left so abruptly after dinner," Howard sneered. "I saw your little layout of napkins on the kitchen table." Howard started toward me. I knew if he closed the door, I'd be in trouble. In a fraction of a second, I began to run at him, throwing my full body weight against him, which, considering his slim build, probably matched his. I knocked him backward, and we both fell into the main hall, a jumble of arms and legs. I got up to run, but he grabbed my shirt. I swung hard at at his arm with one hand and yanked my shirt out of his grasp with the other, which gave me freedom long enough to twist around and take a running step. I felt Howard grab my ankle. I kicked him in the face, feeling contact with a soft spot and kicking off my shoe in the process. He was cursing and writhing on the floor for several seconds, enough to give me a head start.

The only trouble was I was heading the wrong way, to the dead end of the hallway. I would have had to turn and step over Howard to get to the stairway or elevator, and I didn't think he'd lie still for that. I remembered the old hauling elevator. I ran to the end of the hall, grabbed old canvases and frames that leaned against the wall, and threw them behind me, exposing the elevator door. I looked over my shoulder. Howard was trying to stand, his hand covering one eye, blood flowing from his nose. I had to yank several times before the door would budge, but I managed to slide it open sideways, just enough to squeeze in, and threw my weight against it to slide it closed before Howard reached me.

It was a manual dumbwaiter sort of elevator, built for hauling finished bolts of cotton and woolen fabric to the ground level. I grabbed the rope and hauled with all my strength, praying it wouldn't break. The old elevator groaned but began to move. Up. I let go and grabbed the parallel rope, yanked hard, and slowly began to descend. As I passed the glass window in the old wooden door, I was inches from Howard, red faced, screaming and beating on the door with his fists. I'd have to be pretty fast to reach the first floor before he did. Then it hit me: he would be expecting me to go to the first floor and out the front door to the parking lot.

The elevator seemed to creep at a snail's pace, like a dandelion puff making its way to the ground. I passed the first floor and felt a crunching lurch, signaling I had reached the basement. I pulled mightily on the door to get enough room to sidle out. The hallway was dark. There were no windows on the left side since the ground banked up from the parking lot to the first floor above me. The studios along the right side of the hall had windows, but there was no moon tonight and no streetlights on this side, which faced the harbor. I stumbled over some boxes but kept making my way down the hallway, feeling with my hands along the wall. I hit the panic bar on the back door and began running. I was on the park side of the mill, but the relatively flat ground was not so flat when you're running in the dark with one shoe.

I hadn't thought any farther than getting out of the building, so I raced up the inclined ground to the front corner of the building and cautiously peered around, my eyes still adjusting to the darkness. I figured I could make it to my car if Howard wasn't in sight. I kicked off my other shoe and took off in a silent jog across the parking lot, digging my keys out of my pocket in the process. My heart was pounding. If I got through this, I promised myself, I'd increase my runs with Jesse.

I slowed as I neared my car and reached for the door handle. Howard appeared from behind the bumper. He locked onto my arm. I screamed. He spun me around, pinning me against the hatchback. He had blood dripping from his nose or eye, I couldn't tell which. He pulled out a length of rope and slipped it over my wrists, coiling it tightly. He was stronger than he looked. My flailing did not stop him, nor did my screaming.

"Shut up, you bitch!" Howard's voice was scary; it was flat with no emotion. I kneed him in the groin as hard as I could, which to my relief sent him doubling over in pain.

"Laney!" I heard my name called somewhere in the distance, but I could not afford to take my eyes off Howard. This behavior was so unlike him that I was mesmerized, even while I was battling him. Then again, it was apparent that I knew little about what Howard was really like.

Suddenly Rose was by my side, holding on to me tightly, and another, more massive form was leaning over Howard, yanking him to his feet. As they stood up, I was surprised to see it was Michael manhandling Howard. Michael had never looked so welcome.

"You all right?" Michael called over his shoulder.

"Yeah." I pulled at the ropes on my wrists to no avail. Rose pulled out a miniscule Swiss Army knife and began sawing away.

Michael kept one hand gripped firmly on Howard's bicep, his fingers fully encircling it, while he pulled his cell phone out of his pocket and dialed 911 with the other hand.

"Yeah, uh, I've got someone here you're looking for, the suspected murderer of Kalen Farrell. You need to get here stat. Try to make it in less than five minutes this time!" His voice reflected the urgency and irritation that I felt.

Michael shoved Howard against the car and pinned him in with his whole body. A noise that sounded like a whimper escaped from Howard. He didn't seem so strong now.

Michael was yelling into the phone now. "No, don't put me on hold! Look, I just made your lives a whole lot easier. We're at the Hartmann Mill, six blocks from the damn station. Okay. Two minutes." He slid the phone into his pocket.

This time three police cars and a canine unit came peeling in, sirens screaming, all within ninety seconds. There was so much confusion and so many guns drawn, it was almost comical.

"Jesus!" Michael had to move quickly to get out of the line of fire of the shortest cop, in case he got nervous and pulled the trigger. Howard was being shackled and having the Miranda rights shouted at him by another officer, who then secured him in the back seat of one of the police cars.

The tall officer, whom I'm pretty sure I'd met at least once in the last couple of days, took my statement and made me promise to come to the station in the morning to make a full report before he would let me go.

Shakily, I pushed past the open door of the police car. I couldn't keep myself from asking, "Why, Howard?"

He looked up at me, the streetlight glinting off his eyes, "You wouldn't understand. No one would."

He spoke now in a soft monotone. He sounded like he was talking to himself.

"All the things I paint, all my other subjects, even still lifes, have to be improved upon. Get the flaws out. Hide the imperfections. I didn't have to change anything when I painted her. She was perfect, and I intended to keep her that way. I couldn't let her be treated the way Kalen treated her. I heard them a lot through the vent in the floor, you know, arguing."

The police were talking to the station and to Michael and Rose, so I kept Howard talking.

"I was working in my studio late Friday night. The elevator was jammed, so I was bringing a painting down the stairway to put in my car when I heard someone in the hallway on the second floor. I went out to see if it was Catherine. She works late sometimes, you know."

He was shivering now, and speaking in a faraway voice.

"But instead, I saw Kalen. He was going into Elise's studio with a key, so I waited, then went to take a look." Interesting that he viewed

Montgomery Mannequins as Elise's company, and not mine. Even more interesting that it bothered me.

Howard continued, "Kalen wasn't even trying to be quiet in there; I could hear him banging things around. I went in to try to stop him. He was in your clean room, Laney. He turned around when he heard me, and told me to get out! *He* told *me* to get out! He *shoved* me! He pulled out a *knife*!" Howard was living it over again, and having trouble believing it this time, too.

"He tore that pin right off the dress on the mannequin! Catherine's pin! Said he'd show *her* who's boss. I couldn't let him do that to her anymore. I still I had my white gloves in my pocket, so I put them on and grabbed the sword from the figure in the corner. I had to stop him!" Howard was shaking visibly now.

"So you were the one who put the pin back in Rose's shop?" I prodded him gently. It was strange, but now I was feeling sorry for the man who had attacked me ten minutes ago.

"I couldn't let the pin be found in Kalen's hand. Don't you see? That would have led the police right to Catherine. But they came and took Catherine anyway. I didn't think they'd really think she'd murdered Kalen. Not that he didn't deserve it. I would never have let her go to prison."

Couldn't he see that putting the pin back in the case in Vintage Dresses still led the police to Catherine and made her look even guiltier?

"Laney!" came a sharp voice, making me look up with a jerk. "Are you alright? I heard this address on the scanner and prayed it wasn't you." Dale's concerned voice cut through the commotion.

I turned away from Howard and walked over to Dale. How to thank him and also tell him I valued our friendship as it was? I hated that cliché of just wanting to be friends, but it was apropos. He looked at me, then to Michael, then to back to me. He gave me a warm hug and whispered in my ear, "I know." I felt like a heel. I didn't even have to explain. He really was a good guy.

When the police cars carrying Howard and the precinct cops pulled out of the parking lot, I suddenly realized how close I had come to … to what? Death? I crumpled onto the curb when I realized Howard would have killed me. Rose parked herself next to me and put her arm around my shoulders. Michael sat down on the other side of me, and I leaned into him. The warmth of both their bodies was comforting. Nobody said anything for a few moments. I was happy to be alive. I looked up to see Dale surveying the scene. He gave me a knowing look and a sad smile that seemed to say, "I'm glad you're okay, and I get it."

"How did you know it was Howard?" Michael asked.

"It was the key."

"What do you mean?"

"The only way someone could have gotten in to our studio without breaking the door down was if they had a key. I realized it in the kitchen the other day, when Elise and I were talking about spare keys being on

Chester's key ring. I told Elise I'd sort through them, but I didn't get around to it."

Rose explained to Michael that Chester was the Security Guard figure on the second floor outside my studio.

"When I realized there was a possibility that one of the keys might have been an old spare one to our studio, giving anyone access, everything fell into place. I just needed confirmation, so I came down here to see if our key was on the ring. The whole key ring was missing! So I figured that's how Kalen got in. Both times. It made sense; he was looking for the topaz pin. "His" topaz. But it wasn't here the first time he broke in—the night I came back in for Rose's dress; Catherine was still working on it then. I figured that's why the purple iolite pin was missing from Rose's dress when I took it home to alter. He must have thought it was the topaz in the dark. Once he knocked me out, I guess he looked at it and threw it on the table, where I found it the next day."

I was pouring out the sequence of events, trying to make sense of it even to myself.

"But the key wasn't on Kalen's body," I continued, "and the crime scene guys didn't find it anywhere in the clean room, so I figured whoever killed Kalen must have taken it. If I could find the key, I'd find the killer."

"Laney! You damn fool." Michael shook his head. "That was a dangerous thing to do by yourself. Once you realized your studio key might have been on the key ring, you should have called the police. Or at least me."

"I figured I'd come look around tonight while the mill was empty. Then I'd have proof." My reasoning sounded hollow now. "I took Elise's master key and went to look around all the studios." I shook my head and let out a sigh that sounded, even to me, like a sob.

"Oh God! Howard was infatuated with her. Obsessed! His studio is filled with paintings of her." An involuntary shudder made me aware of the chilly night air. That, and that I was sitting on a cold curb in my shirtsleeves, and shoeless.

"How did you know where to find me?" I said in a froggy voice to both of them.

Rose spoke up. "Elise called me. Said you left quickly after dinner without sayin' anything, and Howard hightailed it out with only a meager explanation. Said she didn't have a good feelin' about it. Said since I lived close to the mill, would I drive by and call her if I saw anything?" She chuckled just then. "She wanted me to drive! Can you imagine? I'd'a lost my parking spot in front'a my house!" She elbowed me, and her old familiar grin was back, though her eyes were glassy.

"So I called Michael, since I knew you two were in cahoots." I could swear she winked at me. Her attempt at levity was working. I felt my awareness finally returning.

"Besides," she whispered in my ear, "it was either call him or call Dale to rescue you. And *I'm* no dummy!" Now it was my turn to smile. I leaned into Rose with my shoulder. It was then I looked around to thank Dale again, and saw he had disappeared.

"Laney, let's get you home." Michael's deep, rich voice was low and calm.

"Wait, Michael. There's one thing I need to do first. Come with me if you like."

Michael followed me into the building and up into my studio. We located my figure, the one I'd come to call the Laney figure, and moved it into the front lounge, just inside the door next to Grandpa Albert, to welcome future clients. It was time to bring her out of hiding.

Then we headed home.

About the Author

Penelope Clifton has had the distinct pleasure of spending most of her working life interacting with super-realistic mannequins. She has had the challenge of working first-hand with CEOs, exhibit designers, and famous, and not-so-famous, people whose likenesses now grace museums around the country and beyond. Her hobbies include quilting and repairing antique quilts, reading, and woodturning. She has two grown sons, one granddaughter, and lives in a small town not unlike Carter's Village in the mid-Atlantic region.

Made in the USA
Middletown, DE
26 March 2019